SLIGO

FOLK TALES

JOE MCGOWAN

ILLUSTRATED BY ANNA MCGLOIN

The
History
Press
Ireland

Come, faeries, take me out of this dull house!
Let me have all the freedom I have lost;
Work when I will and idle when I will!
Faeries, come take me out of this dull world,
For I would ride with you upon the wind,
Run on the top of the dishevelled tide,
And dance upon the mountains like a flame.

W.B. Yeats, *The Land of Heart's Desire*

First published 2015

The History Press Ireland
50 City Quay
Dublin 2
Ireland
www.thehistorypress.ie

© Joe McGowan, 2015
Illustrations © Anna McGloin, 2015

The right of Joe McGowan to be identified as the Author
of this work has been asserted in accordance with the
Copyright, Designs and Patents Act 1988.

British Library Cataloguing in Publication Data.
A catalogue record for this book is available from the British Library.

ISBN 978 1 84588 836 7

Typesetting and origination by The History Press

CONTENTS

Acknowledgements

I would like to acknowledge with thanks permissions granted by Críostóir Mac Cárthaigh, archivist of the National Folkore Collection, to include some of the stories reproduced here.

Every effort has been made to trace and contact copyright holders. If there are any inadvertent omissions I apologise to those concerned, and will correct any oversight in subsequent editions.

INTRODUCTION

For the devotee of Irish heritage, mythology or folklore, County Sligo, in the west coast province of Connacht, has everything. For those who take time to read the landscape, every stone and hill has its own unique, often bloody, story to tell. Here one can literally trace the dramatic tendrils of our nation, from mythological origins through a turbulent history to a modern nation. In its lofty mountains, its winding rivers, its jagged coastline, God has created here a land blessed by time and unspoiled by man.

From the Curlew mountains in the south, where Aodh Ruadh Ó Domhnaill defeated an English army under Sir Conyers Clifford, to Benbulben's slopes in the north, where St Colmcille battled the High King of Ireland, every hill and valley is linked by gossamer threads of myth, folklore and history. Keshcorran, birthplace of Cormac Mac Art and home to Diarmuid and Gráinne, is linked to Benbulben, where Diarmuid met his death at the hands of the wild boar.

The mighty prow of 'bare Benbulben's head', made famous by the poet W.B. Yeats, defines the County Sligo landscape. This is 'Yeats' country', a countryside rich in history, folklore and mythology. In Drumcliffe churchyard, the poet himself lies at peace in the Sligo soil that inspired much of his work.

The ancient bards and *filidh* were respected and highly valued. Their verses and tales were told in Tara's halls; their memories the repositories of great deeds of the Irish race and treasured epics like 'The Song of Amhergan' and the '*Táin Bó Cúailnge*'. They cherished the ancient sagas

passed on from generation to generation through the mists of pre-history until they were written down by the early Christian monks. Sometimes it was almost too late. The chief *filidhe,* Senchan Torpeist, endeavoured to gather together the elements of the *Táin* in the reign of Guaire Aidne, the seventh-century King of Connacht. Along with his son, Muirgen, he called up the spirit of the dead hero Fergus to help them with their task.

Men like Henry Conway of Carns, County Sligo, or Jimmy McGettrick of Ballymote, County Sligo, would dismiss any accolades or tributes to their talent. Yet their contribution to our knowledge of things past is as great as the men who memorised the *Táin,* their minds a repository of tales and verse, comic and sad, of the glories of the Gael. Henry's was no bardic school, but a modest fireside where he pitted his intelligence against Roger Moore of Drumfad in verse and storytelling feats. The storytellers' knowledge, tempered by their own experience, was handed down to them by men and women of another generation.

Out of the treasure chest of his mind Henry drew for me the 'Ballad of Pat Donlevy,'[1] a song and story of treachery and deceit remembered from Land League days over 100 years before. Without his scholarship and interest, the story of this hero of another age would have been consigned to that vast black hole with so much that has already been already lost. Without any prompting he would launch into classics like 'The Burial of Sir John Moore at *Corunna*':

Not a drum was heard, not a funeral note,
As his corpse to the rampart we hurried;
Not a soldier discharged his farewell shot
O'er the grave where our hero we buried.

We buried him darkly at dead of night,
The sods with our bayonets turning;
By the struggling moonbeam's misty light
And the lantern dimly burning …

Poaching, rebellion, smuggling; these were not crimes here in the chimney corner, but rights. Ernie O'Malley wrote of long nights spent with such people during his time on the run during the War of Independence:

Here was their paper, a living warp and weft spun of their own thoughts, fancies and doings. Now and again a biting turn of phrase, for in their nature was the old Gaelic satire … there was a love of discussion and argument that would take up a subject casually without belief and in a searching way develop it … Deferential to a stranger, they evoked in themselves a sympathetic mood, changing gears in conversation to suit his beliefs and half believing then through sympathy whilst he was present. Afterwards when they checked up on themselves it might be different; they would laugh at the strangers' outlandish opinions when their mood hardened.

Michael Collins, another hero of the War of Independence, wrote that:

Great age held something for me that was awesome. I was much fonder of the old people in the darkness than I was of the young people in the daytime. It's at night that you're able to get the value of old people. And it was listening to the old people that I got my idea of Irish nationality.

A gesture of the hand, a facial expression drew pictures from words. The listeners looked into the flames and, aided by these spell weavers, saw there the clamour and conflict, the fire of ancient battles: Fionn's pursuit of Diarmuid and Gráinne, the *Táin Bó Cúailnge*, Granuaile's exploits.

Many of the fireside *seanchaidhe*, survivors of a crucible of conquest and colonisation, were men who had little or no formal education. Yet, in the manner of the bards of long ago, they could commit to memory endless anecdotes, stories, riddles and legends. Their minds were a treasure house of lore and tradition, inspiring a unique and natural-born talent that could never be acquired. They possessed a simplicity and authenticity, a cadence, rhythm and sense of timing that formal education would have destroyed.

'There might be seven or eight people in a rambling house,' Mickey McGroarty recalled.

'Twas all clay pipes was goin' that time. They'd fill the pipe and when one man had a good smoke on it, he'd pull his fingers on the shank and pass it on to the man beside him. When he'd have a smoke he'd pull his fingers on it an' pass it on to the next man an' so on till every man had a good smoke. All ye had to do was fill one pipe in the night because every man took a turn filling his pipe an' passing it on. When the seven or eight pipes was filled ye had a big night's smoking done – the one pipe gave every man a smoke. The baccy that's goin' today, it's not baccy at all, ye haven't it lit till it's gone!

The night was no time in passin' with all the different stories ye'd hear. I learned them all from the oul' people. I learnt it an' I drunk it by heart. When I was goin' home on a dark winter's night I was going over the story in me mind the same way the oul' people told it. Even when I went to bed, before the sleep took me, I'd be trying to remember what I heard from the oul' men. The next day I had it off be heart.

Outside the camaraderie of that comforting fireside circle, in the murky, dimly lit corners of the kitchen, phantasmal ancestors long passed away listened unseen in the shadows. Spirits, that once had a place by the fire-lit circle of mortals, loitered where the dancing flames of the burning turf fire and pallid glow of the oil lamp faded into gloom. Overhead where the light strove to penetrate the dim-lit recesses around the smoke-blackened purlins were concealed creatures that crept away only with the dawn light. Flickering flame-thrown shadows of the fireside company danced with phantom visitors on the whitewashed wall, bringing our two worlds into a shadowy unison. Stories of banshees that wailed to foretell a death, desperate struggles with ghosts on lonely paths; anything became possible as we flirted with the spirit-peopled otherworld that from time to time crossed over darkly to ours.

For centuries, the old ways and the old world endured. It was imbedded in the storytellers' souls. More than spectators, they were what they believed, they lived what they told. But their practices and customs collided with a rapidly evolving world. In a clash of traditions, they have lost. Or so it seems. Time will prove the greater loss is ours. In a conflict as profound in its effect as when the Milesians drove the *Tuatha De Danaan* to their underground places, so too the new technology defeated the gentler ways. Mass communication and instant entertainment have obliterated customs and beliefs long held. They have vanished like snow, today glistening white, tomorrow silently and swiftly gone.

The English poet and Celtic scholar Robin Flower once wrote:

> It is only by a glint of colour here, a salient thread there, in the dulled material, that we who strive to reconstitute something of the intricate harmony wrought into the original fabric can imagine to ourselves the bright hues and gay lines of the forgotten past. The world has turned to another way of life, and no passion of regret can revive a dying memory.

Visitors to country kitchens, following the arrival of television, saw that the same people who used to sit around the walls of the kitchen to sing, dance and hear stories now sat on the same chairs and *furms* (long stools) watching whatever flickered on the hypnotic screen.

Mickey McGroarty, Maggie McGowan, Bernie Kelly, Jimmy McGettrick: they and their stories will soon be history. The 'intricate harmony' is no more and the world a poorer place for its going.

Unfolded here then are the beliefs of ordinary people, their superstitions, customs and way of life. Our journey reveals that the character of Ireland, and County Sligo in particular, is a microcosm not just of Sligo, but of a romantic Ireland on the verge of extinction. These stories bring to life the stories, customs and superstitions once told around the fireside at night. The warp and weft of everyday people, their existence mostly unrecognised and unsung, is celebrated in these pages.

1

BALOR AND THE BATTLES OF MOYTURRA

'The Land of Heart's Desire' is how the poet W.B. Yeats described Sligo. And who can argue? It must have always seemed so, starting with the first land-hungry colonists who viewed Benbulben's lofty towers from the wild Atlantic to the O'Neill and the O'Donnell of a later time. 'Yes this is the Promised Land,' we can hear them say. 'Here is a land worth fighting for.'

Who then were the first settlers? What do we know of them? Who were these early ancestors whose blood enriches our veins? What language did they speak?

Our earliest history was memorised, not written. The repositories of this early lore were members of a powerful and privileged caste of poets, diviners and seers in early Ireland. Trained for at least twelve years in rigorous mental exercise, they committed all history and mythology to memory.

Written Celtic tradition is inspired and informed by this learned class of *filidhe* and found in the great collections of manuscripts compiled in monasteries and castles from AD 800 to the time of the transcription of the Annals of the Four Masters in 1632. Their authenticity is disputed, but it will serve us well to remember that although the shaft of sunlight striking the inner chamber at Newgrange was common knowledge locally, it wasn't 'discovered' by the academic world until the early 1960s.

The 'Book of Invasions' (*Leabhair Gabhala*) is one of our earliest sources of information. A twelfth-century text transcribed by Christian monks from identifiable poets of the ninth and tenth centuries, as well as from oral lore, it is an invaluable record. The book is one of the oldest mythologies of the western world and made huge tracts of history available in written form for the first time.

Let us find the first immigrants from another early source, the *Chronicum Scotorum* compiled by Duald McFirbis at Lecan in the Barony of Tireragh. In the year 'Anno Mundi[2] 1599', he says, 'The daughter of one of the Greeks came to Hibernia, whose name was Cesair, and fifty maidens and three men with her.'

Lucky men!

Those eminent chroniclers, the Four Masters, agree with McFirbis: 'Forty days before the Deluge, Ceasair came to Ireland with fifty girls and three men – Bith, Ladhra and Fintain, their names.' The group evidently hadn't bothered to take a place in Noah's Ark! Coming to Ireland was an inspired choice though, as they seem to have escaped the fate that overcame the rest of the world. Of these early colonists we know little else.

We have somewhat more information on the Parthalonians or Scythians, who arrived in Ireland in AM 2520 or, as it is calculated, 278 years after the Deluge or, if you like, the twenty-first year of the age of the Patriarch Abraham as recorded in the Annals. To put the timescale in context, the ancients placed the Deluge at 1,656 years after the Creation. Let's just simplify things and say it was around 1500 BC.

Parthalon's followers are also said to have come from Greece. Perhaps they were looking for Cesair and her handmaidens, who had sailed out on uncharted seas many years before. We don't know. The Fomorians arrived some few years after this but were roundly defeated by Parthalon and his men. However, the Parthalonians scarcely had time to savour the fruits of their victory before they were wiped out by a plague. The sound of a human voice was not heard in Ireland again until the arrival, in AM 2859, of the Nemedians.

According to Geoffrey Keating's *History of Ireland*, the leader of this group, Nemedius, was eleventh in descent from Noah. Settling in Maugherow, north of Sligo town, they enjoyed undisputed tenancy for over two centuries. Maugherow at that time comprised all of the area between the Benbulben range and the sea.

The Fomorians, however, after a long absence, stormed onto the scene once again. They had somewhat more success this time as by the year

AM 3060 they had succeeded in founding settlements in Sligo and other points along the west coast. Establishing their principal stronghold on Tory Island off the Donegal coast, they were the bad boys of this prehistoric era. According to historian Revd E.A. D'Alton, they lived, 'by piracy and plunder of other nations, and were very troublesome to the whole world.' We can imagine how ordinary decent Nemedians must have felt about this: 'There goes the neighbourhood,' we can hear them say.

But worse was yet to come. An even worse band of villains in the form of the Firbolgs (literally 'bagmen') arrived in AM 3266. Sligo must have been high on a list of places to conquer in the Greek War Office then, as these latest arrivals were Scythians as well. 'Black, loquacious, lying, tale bearing and of low grovelling mind' is how they are described in the *Book of Lecan*. Seventeenth-century Sligo historian Duald Mac Firbis described the Firbolgs as black haired, thieving and churlish and for good measure threw in 'mean and contemptible' as well! Establishing their chief seats of power at Tara and Sligo, they quickly conquered Connacht and extended their rule as far as Meath and Leinster.

The Firbolgs had it their own way for only about forty years, when the *Tuatha De Danaan* arrived. They came off a bit better in Mac Firbis's description, which characterised them as fair haired and skilful, but nevertheless they were also plunderers, large and vengeful. They were as fair of skin and feature as the previous invaders were dark. Immediately on arriving on Sligo shores, we are told, they burnt their boats. The Firbolgs didn't spot them until they got as far as Leitrim and, seeing no boats, attributed their arrival to some form of magic. Magic was big in Ireland then, so this perception gave the newcomers an advantage right away.

The Firbolgs sent their best warrior, Sreng, to a meeting with Breas, his counterpart on the *De Danaan* side. The two ambassadors examined each other's weapons with great interest. The spears of the *De Danaans* were apparently light and sharp-pointed, those of the Firbolgs heavy and blunt. Breas sued for peace, making the very reasonable point that Ireland was big enough and couldn't they divide it between them? Sreng brought the offer back to his leader King Eochy who, encouraged by Sreng's evaluation of the invaders' strength, immediately declared war on King Nuada of the *De Danaan*.

They, hoping to avoid a confrontation, retreated to Moyturra near Cong in County Mayo. The Firbolgs followed and, despite peace feelers by King Nuada who was reluctant to fight, the battle commenced. King Eochy was immediately thrown into confusion when he couldn't even find his opponents. The *De Danaan* had caused a magical mist to descend on their camp, concealing them completely from view. When the battle eventually began, it lasted for four days, at the end of which the Firbolgs were destroyed and their numbers reduced to 300 men. The *De Danaan* pursued the fleeing enemy to Beltra strand near Ballisodare in County Sligo. Here they administered the *coup de grace* when they killed King Eochy. This great battle, known as the First Battle of Moyturra, is said to have happened around 2,000 BC, 700 years before the Siege of Troy.

Following the battle, a truce was called and an agreement made: the Firbolgs would take the province of Connacht for their territory, while the *De Danaans* would take the rest of Ireland. The possibility that the Firbolgs did in fact at one time exist is mooted by the scholar Mac Firbis who, in his seventeenth-century investigations, proposed that the ancestry of many of the inhabitants of Connacht could be traced to these same Firbolgs.

Some time after this conflict, a rift developed between the warrior hero Breas and his *De Danaan* comrades. Breas fled to the Hebrides to seek assistance from his Fomorian relatives, who ruled there. Assembling an invasion force and, placing it under the leadership of Balor of the Evil Eye, they sailed for Sligo.

Described as a man of 'gigantic size and Herculean strength' Balor was 'perfectly skilled in the Magic Art, he always kept a cover on his eye which he took off whenever he intended to do an injury by his look'. The power was said to have come from a druid cauldron; left to guard the mixture, Balor had lifted the lid and was sprayed by the vapour escaping from the boiling pot. Afterwards, imbued by a magical power, whole armies could be struck down with one glance of his eye. A perfect match, it seems, for the *De Danaan* who, up until now, had it all their own way in the magic department.

Balor may have been the first in Ireland with the curse of the Evil Eye. In a less fearful fashion, 'blinking' or the 'overlook' has existed from the dawn of history into modern times. Jealous or resentful people are

said to have the power to do harm just by casting their eyes on stock or property. It is respected and feared not just in Ireland, but in world folklore as well. The poet W.B. Yeats, remarking on the phenomenon, said that: 'the admired and desired are only safe if one says, "God bless them when one's eyes are upon them".'

Landing at Ballisodare, Balor, the disgruntled Breas, and an army of men marched to Moyturra in the parish of Kilmactranny, Barony of Tirerrill. This plain is 700ft high and 1 square mile with valleys on three sides and Lough Arrow to the west. It is remarkable to this day for the number of sepulchral monuments, pillars, monoliths and obelisks, that exist there. These groups were soon joined by remnants of the previously defeated Firbolgs, anxious for revenge. It was payback time! Space does not allow the battle to be described here in full but the Tuathas were fearsome opponents.

Lugh was chosen to lead the *Tuatha De Danaan* into battle against the Fomorians and their champion, Balor. The battle began on the Feast of Samhain with some preliminary skirmishes, in which the Fomorians got a rude awakening when they experienced the superior weaponry of the *De Danaan* and their ability to restore the wounded to health:

> Fearful indeed was the thunder which rolled over the battlefield; the shouts of the warriors, the breaking of the shields, the flashing and clashing of the swords, of the straight, ivory-hilted swords, the music and harmony of the 'belly-darts' and the sighing and winging of the spears and lances.

> The *Tuatha De Danaan*
> By force of potent spells and wicked magic,
> And conjurations horrible to bear –
> Could set the ministers of hell at work
> And raise a slaughtered army from the earth –
> And make them live and breathe and fight again …
> (T.W. Rolleston, *Myths and Legends of the Celtic Race*)

As the battle proceeded, there was great slaughter on both sides. The annals relate that 100,000 men fought and died on the battlefield at Moyturra for possession of the 'Land of Heart's Desire'. The slain of the Fomorians remained so, but those of the *De Danaan* were cast into a well over which the healer Dian Cécht and his three children sang spells and, by its magic, they were restored to life. Lugh also used his powers, moving around his army on one foot and with one eye he chanted an incantation to lend them strength and courage. He thus assumed the traditional posture of the sorcerer and one that was attributed to the Fomhoire.

The hard-pressed Fomorians brought on their champion, Balor, with his venomous fiery eye, on which there was always kept seven coverings. One by one, Balor removed the coverings:

With the first covering the bracken began to wither, with the second the grass was scorched, with the third the woods and timber began to heat, with the fourth smoke came from the trees until with the seventh they were set afire and the whole countryside in a blaze.

In *Gods and Fighting Men*, Lady Gregory describes the battle thus:

And it was a hard battle was fought, and for a while it was going against the *Tuatha De Danaan*; and Nuada of the Silver Hand, their King, and Macha, daughter of Emmass, fell by Balor, King of the Fomor. And Cassmail fell by Octriallach, and the Dagda got a dreadful wound from a casting spear that was thrown by Ceithlenn, wife of Balor.

But when the battle was going on, Lugh broke away from those that were keeping him, and rushed out to the front of the Men of Dea. And then there was a fierce battle fought, and Lugh was heartening the men of Ireland to fight well, the way they would not be in bonds any longer. For it was better for them, he said, to die protecting their own country than to live under bonds and under tribute any longer. And he sang a song of courage to them, and the hosts gave a great shout as they went into battle, and then they met together, and each of them began to attack the other.

And there was great slaughter, and laying low in graves, and many comely men fell there in the stall of death. Pride and shame were there side by side, and hardness and red anger, and there was red blood on the white skin of young fighting men. And the dashing of spear against shield, and sword against sword, and the shouting of the fighters, and the whistling of casting spears and the rattling of scabbards was like harsh thunder through the battle. And many slipped in the blood that was under their feet, and they fell, striking their heads one against another; and the river carried away bodies of friends and enemies together.

And as to the number of men that fell in the battle, it will not be known till we number the stars of the sky, or flakes of snow, or the dew on the grass, or grass under the feet of cattle, or the horses of the Son of Lir in a stormy sea.

Then Lugh and Balor met in the battle, and Lugh called out reproaches to him; and there was anger on Balor, and he said to the men that were with him: 'Lift up my eyelid higher till I see this chatterer that is taunting me.'

Then they raised Balor's eyelid, but Lugh quickly made a cast of his red spear at him, that brought the eye out through the back of his head, so that it was towards his own army it fell, and three times nine of the Fomorians died when they looked at it. And if Lugh had not put out that eye when he did, the whole of Ireland would have been burned in one flash. And after this, Lugh struck his head off.

One legend tells that, when Balor was slain by Lugh, his eye was still open as he fell face first on to the ground. His deadly stare burned a hole into the earth from which the blood gushed forth to form a lake which is now known as *Loch na Súl*, or 'Lake of the Eye', which is still to be found in the parish of Kilmactranny.

2

A WILFUL
SAINT

It is well known that St Colmcille, in addition to the establishment of a monastery at Drumcliffe, County Sligo, founded a monastery on Iona in AD 563. What is not so well known is that it was St Molaise of Inishmurray, a small island off the coast of County Sligo, that was responsible for Colmcille's exile and odyssey to Iona. It is no small matter, for the foundation of Iona is credited with being the inspiration for a wave of missionary zeal that eventually brought learning, culture and religion to a barbarised Europe.

Molaise was confessor to St Colmcille and it was to him that this holy man went in great remorse after the Battle of *Cúl Dreimhne* (anglicised to Cooldrumman) in North Sligo. This 'Battle of the Books' came about when Colmcille copied one of St Finian's manuscripts that he had admired and subsequently borrowed. Although there is no historical proof, we believe the book in question may have been the *Cathac*. Others say it was the text of the chronicle of Rufinus of Aquileia, which is known to have been brought to Ireland in the fifth century and used subsequently on Iona in the monastery established by Colmcille.

Lending books, even in modern times, has its pitfalls. The sixth century, it turns out, was no different – even when it was saints that were involved. When St Colmcille returned the original he refused, much to Finian's chagrin, to give up the copy as well. Arguing that he had returned what he had borrowed and that the copy belonged to him, the dispute escalated between the two holy men until it was eventually brought to the High King of Ireland, Diarmuit Mac Cerrbhéll, for adjudication. The king, having considered the matter, issued his now famous edict, reputed to be the first ever recorded copyright judgement: *'Le gach boin a boinín is le gach leabhar a leabhrán.'* (To every cow its calf and to every book its copy.)

Remaining resolute and unmoved, Colmcille stubbornly refused to obey the ruling. In consequence of the saint's refusal the armies of the High King and Colmcille, in AD 561, fought a pitched battle on the slopes of Benbulben Mountain in County Sligo. Thousands were slain, Colmcille was victorious and the king forced to concede the copy of the Psalter to the victor.

Despite his triumph, Colmcille's conscience bothered him and he was soon stricken by remorse for his defiance and the slaughter he had caused. Molaise of Inishmurray was his confessor and it was to him that this holy man then went in order to confess his sin. The *Martyrology of Donegal* records that they met at the cross of *Ath Iomlaise* (Ahamlish) situated near the well of St Molaise at the entrance to Ahamlish grave-yard near Grange village. They were blood relations as Colmcille's sister, Cumenia, was St Molaise's mother.

St Molaise's Well, still in existence but now fallen into disuse, was much visited until recent years because of its curative properties. In the last nineteenth century the volume of pilgrims was a source of great annoyance to a Protestant clergyman who lived nearby. The landlord, Lord Palmerston, closed the well at the minister's request. To his dismay, when the minister came downstairs the next morning, the well had sprung up in his living room. He went immediately to Palmerston, who ordered his workmen to restore the well upon which the parson's home returned to normal.

Island tradition holds that it was not at Ahamlish, but at Inishmurray that the meeting between Molaise and Colmcille took place. It is said that when Colmcille went to Stáid Abbey at Streedagh in order to cross over to Inishmurray to confess his sins, there was no boat available. Not to be deterred by such a trifle, he threw his cloak on the water and a green path immediately opened before him. Just as with the parting of the Red Sea at Moses' command, Colmcille then walked across to Inishmurray. Ever since that time, no harm has ever come to any boat

travelling to or from Inishmurray that way. It is a fact that while the
islanders lived on Inishmurray it was firmly held that, regardless of sea
swell or storm, no boat travelling on this path ever came to harm.

As a result of the meeting with Molaise, Colmcille's penance was to leave
Ireland, never to see or put foot on the island again and to win as many
souls for God as were lost in the battle at *Cúl Dreimhne*. Colmcille was
distraught at having to leave the land of his birth that he loved so much:

> Broken is my heart in its breast;
> Should sudden death overtake me
> It is for my great love of the Gael …

> … Were all Alba mine
> From its centre to the border
> I would rather have the site of a house
> In the middle of fair Derry …

Sailing with a heavy heart to Iona in AD 563, he was one of a wave of
Irish missionaries that colonised a barbarised Europe, bringing learning,
culture and religion with them. Scots, Picts, Irish, Britons and Anglo-
Saxons poured into Iona to learn at Colmcille's feet. 'While Rome and
its ancient empire faded from memory and a new, illiterate Europe rose
on its ruins, a vibrant, literary culture was blooming in secret along its
Celtic fringe', Thomas Cahill wrote.[3]

Before his death at the end of the sixth century, Colmcille's disci-
ples had founded sixty monastic communities in Scotland. From there,
learning and Christianity spread to the pagan Angles of Lindisfarne and
Northumbria. Uncontainable, faith and learning spilled on from there
to continental Europe.

The stones, clochauns and churches of Inishmurray speak to us today
of the richness and diversity of our great cultural heritage, of a land once
called the 'Island of Saints and Scholars'. If it weren't for the penance
imposed on Colmcille by St Molaise of Inishmurray, Iona would have
remained an obscure and desolate outpost on the edge of the civilised
world - and the history of the Christianisation of Europe been written
differently, if at all.

3

CORMAC
MAC AIRT

Cormac Mac Airt (son of Art) was the most celebrated of all the High Kings of Ireland. His reign, according to medieval historians, is said to have been from AD 204 to 244. He is said to have ruled from Tara, the seat of the High Kings of Ireland, for all those years, and under his rule, it flourished. He was famous for his wise, true, and generous judgments. In the *Annals of Clonmacnoise*, translated in 1627, he is described as: 'absolutely the best king that ever reigned in Ireland ... wise learned, valiant and mild, not given causelessly to be bloody as many of his ancestors were, he reigned majestically and magnificently'.

Although a famous High King, his beginnings were humble and troubled. Cormac's father was the High King, Art Mac Cuinn. His mother was Achtan, daughter of Olc Acha, a smith (or druid) from Connacht. According to the saga *The Battle of Mag Mucrama*, Olc gave Art hospitality the night before the Battle of Maigh Mucruimhe. It had been prophesied that a great progeny would come from Olc's line, so he offered the High King his daughter to sleep with. That night Cormac was conceived.

Achtan had a vision as she slept next to Art. She saw herself with her head cut off and a great tree growing out of her neck. Its branches spread all over Ireland, until the sea rose and overwhelmed it. Another tree grew from the roots of the first, but the wind blew it down. At that she woke up and told Art what she had seen. Art explained that the head of every woman is her husband, and that she would lose her husband in battle the next day.

The first tree was their son, who would be king over all Ireland, and the sea that overwhelmed it was a fish bone that would cause him to choke to death. The second tree was his son, Cairbre Lifechair, who would be king after him, and the wind that blew him down was a battle against the Fianna, in which he would fall. The following day Art was indeed defeated and killed by his nephew Lughaidh Mac Con, who became the new High King.

Achtan fled towards Connacht along with her servant, hoping to gain the protection of Art's brother-in-law, Lughna. Losing their way in the woods near the Caves of Keash, they stopped near a well still known as Cormac's Well. Here Achtan went into labour and gave birth to the baby Cormac within the chariot in which she travelled. They made a bed of leaves and moss for the baby and in the morning, Achtan sent her servant away in search of Lughna. The day was warm and soon the mother nodded off and fell into a deep sleep. Awaking with a start, she turned to nurse the child – but it wasn't there. It had disappeared while she slept.

Some hours later, the servant returned with Lughna and his men with the intention of bringing the mother and child to his residence. Shocked and distressed when they heard what had happened, they immediately scoured the countryside – but the boy could not be found anywhere. A reward was offered for any information that would lead to the recovery of the child, dead or alive. Weeks went by, and months, until eventually they gave up hope. The child surely must be dead or carried away to some remote corner of Ireland.

Seven years went by until one day swineherds minding pigs noticed wolves at play near the caves of Keash. There was nothing unusual about that as the caves were a known haunt for wolves. However, on close obser-vation, the swineherds noticed an unusual animal among them. It looked different to the others, almost human they thought, as it went about on all fours like the wolves. Could it be the lost child? Was the reward still to be had for his recovery? They would find out and immediately set about making a plan to distract the wolves and grab the strange human-like figure.

Lighting a fire on the brow of the hill and to the west, they put a pig to roast on it. The wind was blowing towards the caves so they were hoping the wolf pack would be drawn to the scent. Withdrawing to nearby bushes, the swineherds soon observed the wolves with their heads in the air, sniffing and yelping and coming closer and closer to the pig roast.

The strange creature was not with them. It had fallen behind and the
swineherds, seizing the opportunity, grabbed the creature, and took it
with them. It scratched and clawed and screeched at them but still they
could see it was, to be sure, a human child.

Carrying it triumphantly to Lughna, they claimed their prize. Even though it crawled on all fours and could only growl, yelp and whine like a wolf, Lughna and Achtan were convinced that it was indeed Cormac, the lost child. From then on it was reared in the chief's house in the hope that the child would grow up to succeed his father. With time and patience, the young boy talked and walked like a normal child and went on eventually to become one of the most illustrious High Kings of Ireland, reigning for forty years.

The prophecy was fulfilled – even to the manner of his death, immortalised in verse by Samuel Ferguson. 'The Burial of King Cormac' records the anger, and revenge, of the Pagan priesthood at Cormac's conversion to Christianity and his rejection of the pagan god Crom Cruach.

'Crom Cruach and his sub-gods twelve,'
said Cormac, 'are but carven treene;
The axe that made them, haft or helve,
Had worthier of our worship been …'

… Anon to priests of Crom was brought –
Where, girded in their service dread,
They minister'd on red Moy Sleacht –
Word of the words King Cormac said.

They loosed their curse against the King;
They cursed him in his flesh and bones;
And daily in their mystic ring
They turn'd their maledictive stones,

Till, where at meat the monarch sate,
Amid the revel and the wine,
He choked upon the food he ate
At Sletty, southward of the Boyne …

Most of the stories of the Fenian Cycle are set during Cormac's reign, during which time the hero Fionn Mac Cumhaill is said to have lived.

4

DIARMUID AND GRÁINNE

The legend of Diarmuid and Gráinne rivals any of the great love stories of the world: Antony and Cleopatra, Heloise and Abelard, Lancelot and Guinevere. Predating the twelfth-century tale of Tristan and Iseult, it influenced the Arthurian romance of Lancelot and Guinevere. It incorporates all the ingredients to lift the reader out of our own ordinary everyday lives: love, hate, treachery, deception, murder. No matter where you go in Ireland, you will still find somewhere claiming to be Diarmuid and Gráinne's bed, where the infatuated pair are said to have lain in their fugitive flight. The tragic climax to the affair takes place in County Sligo on the slopes of Benbulben Mountain.

The story begins with the ageing Fionn, leader of a warrior band known as the Fianna, grieving over the death of his wife Maignes. Sitting on a hillside at daybreak in Almu in Leinster, two of his followers approached him: Oisin, Fionn's son, along with his friend Diorruing, the son of Dobhar O'Baoiscne. According to P.W. Joyce's account in *Ancient Celtic Romances*, Oisin enquired of Fionn why he was up so early:

'I am without a wife since Maignes, the daughter of Garad Mac Moirne, died, for he does not slumber nor sleep so well who happens to be without a fitting wife. That is why I am up so early, Oisin.

'I myself could find for you a wife and a mate,' Diorruing volunteered.

'Who is she?' said Fionn.

'She is Gráinne, the daughter of Cormac Mac Art, the son of Conn of the Hundred Battles,' said Diorruing.

'By my hand, Diorruing,' replied Fionn, 'there has been strife and bad blood between Cormac and myself for a long time. If he refuses me the hand of his daughter, it would be an unforgiveable insult. I want you both to go to ask the marriage of his daughter for me of Cormac, for I could better endure a refusal of marriage to be given to you than to myself.'

The two warriors went immediately to Tara, where Cormac, High King of Ireland, gave the two men a friendly welcome. The two men explained the reason for their visit and Cormac replied: 'There is not a son of a king or of a great prince, a hero or a battle-champion in Erin, to whom my daughter has not given refusal of marriage, and it is on me that everyone lays the blame. I will not give you any formal decision until ye yourselves go before my daughter, for it is better that ye hear her own words than that ye be displeased with me.'

After that, the two men went to the dwelling where the women were. Cormac sat in on the meeting and he said: 'Here, my daughter, are two of the people of Fionn Mac Cumhaill coming to ask you as wife and as mate for him. It is your decision, how would you like to answer?'

Gráinne, having thought about it had already, made up her mind what she would do: 'If he be a fitting son-in-law for thee, why should he not be a fitting husband and mate for me?' she replied.

The two men returned and on hearing the good news, Fionn set about planning a trip to Tara to celebrate the engagement with his armies and followers. This was a demonstration to impress the inhabitants of the royal residence of his power and influence and his suitability as a husband to the High King's daughter. On arrival at Tara, Cormac met them with his own entourage of chiefs and the nobility of Ireland at that time. According to P.W. Joyce in *Ancient Celtic Romances*:

A gentle welcome was had for Fionn and all the Fianna, and after that they went to the king's mirthful house called Midcuart. The king of Erin sat down to enjoy drinking and pleasure, with his wife at his left shoulder, that is, Eitche, the daughter of Atan of Corcaigh, and Gráinne at her shoulder, and Fionn Mac Cumaill at the king's right hand; and Cairbre Liffecairth son of Cormac sat at one side of the same royal house, and Oisin the son of Fionn at the other side, and each one of them sat according to his rank and to his patrimony from that down.

The druid Daire Duanach Mac Morna was there too, 'and it was not long before there arose gentle talking and mutual discourse between himself and Gráinne'.

All going well here, I hear you say, and indeed it looks like the scene is set for everyone to live happily ever after. However, as those of us who have travelled love's perilous path know too well, and as Lysander noted to Hermia in Shakespeare's *A Midsummer Night's Dream*: 'the course of true love never did run smooth.' This is now where Gráinne throws a spanner in the works.

Cormac may have been impressed with Fionn's show of power and wealth, but Gráinne, seeing that Fionn was older than she had imagined, and having spotted Fionn's two fine strong sons, had a change of heart. 'What is the reason wherefore Fionn is come to this place tonight?' she enquired innocently of the druid, Daire. Daire wasn't a druid for nothing and had an answer ready.

'If thou knowest not that,' said he, 'it is no wonder that I know it not.' But Gráinne was cute enough for him and persisted until she got an answer: 'I desire to learn it of thee,' she replied.

'Well then,' said the wise old druid, 'it is to ask thee as wife and as mate that Fionn is come to this place tonight.'

Gráinne had her eye on Oisin and responded, 'It is a great marvel to me that it is not for Oisin that Fionn asks me, for it were fitter to give me such as he, than a man that is older than my father.'

'Say not that,' said the druid, 'for were Fionn to hear thee, he himself would not have thee, neither would Oisin dare to take thee.'

Then she spotted Diarmuid: 'Who is that freckled, sweet-worded man, upon whom is the curling dusky-black hair and the two red ruddy cheeks, upon the left hand of Oisin, the son of Fionn?' she enquired.

'That man is Diarmuid the grandson of Duibhne, the white-toothed, of the lightsome countenance; that is, the best lover of women and of maidens that is in the whole world,' replied the druid.

Now the fat was in the fire, as Diarmuid's reputation as a lover was well deserved. His charm came from a magical encounter he had with a woman one night while out hunting. It transpired that she was an enchanted member of the *sidhe*, the personification of youth. After sleeping with him, she put a magical love spot on his right cheek that

had the effect of causing any woman looking on it to fall instantly in love
with him. Gráinne was enraptured, forgot all about Oisin, and hatched
a plan to have Diarmuid for herself. As the guest of honour, she persuaded Fionn, her fiancé, and the guests to have a drink in honour of
the occasion. Except for the goblet that was given to Diarmuid, all the
drinks were drugged. No sooner had they taken a draught out of it than
there fell upon all of them a stupor of sleep.

Approaching Diarmuid, Gráinne said to him: 'Wilt thou receive
courtship from me, O'Duibhne?'

'I will not,' said Diarmuid, 'for whatever woman is betrothed to
Fionn, I may not take her.'

'Then,' said Gráinne, 'I put you under taboos of mighty druidism,
Diarmuid, that is, you must take me out of this household tonight, ere
Fionn and the king arise out of that sleep.'

'Evil bonds are those under which thou hast laid me,' said Diarmuid,
'and why have you laid those taboos upon me before all the sons of kings
and of high princes in the king's house this night. It is a wonder that
thou should give me your love instead of Fionn, seeing that there is not
in Erin a man that is fonder of a woman than he. And anyway you must
know, Gráinne, that Fionn has the keys of Tara, and so we cannot leave
even if we wanted to.'

Gráinne had an answer for this too: 'There is a wicket gate to my
bower,' said she, 'and we will pass out through it.'

The pair fled from Tara – and the inevitable wrath of Cormac and
Fionn Mac Cumhaill. Arriving on the banks of the River Shannon at a
place called *Doire Dá Bhaoth*, Diarmuid built them a small hut for shelter,
the first of many 'beds' in which they would sleep as fugitives over the
next seven years.

Livid with anger, it wasn't long until Fionn set out on their trail. He felt
not just betrayed; his pride was deeply wounded at being made a mockery
of in front of all the men of Ireland assembled at Tara. In this way began
the long and torturous pursuit by Fionn of Diarmuid and Gráinne.
Fionn had an advantage in that he had seers that could tell him the
hidden things, such as, in this instance, where the fugitives were hiding.
Once he knew this it would be easy to capture them and have retribution
for the manner in which he was wronged. Fionn too was possessed of

two attributes, gained after he tasted the magical Salmon of Knowledge caught in *Tobar Segais* (Well of Wisdom) near the River Boyne. These were the gift of foreknowledge, and the power of healing from sickness or wounds by giving a drink of water from his cupped hands. Knowing this, and in order to throw their pursuers off the track, Diarmuid and Gráinne slept on a bed of heather when sheltering by the shore and on sea sand when on the mountains.

When they first eloped Diarmuid, out of respect for Fionn, did not
sleep with Gráinne. Gráinne, although not pleased with this outcome,
bided her time and said nothing until one day when, on crossing a
stream, a spurt of water splashed on her leg. Turning to Diarmuid, she
mocked him, saying that the water was bolder than he was. This was
too much for Diarmuid, who in any event being a man of normal
desires, had trouble keeping faith with Fionn. It was following this that
they became lovers. Diarmuid then threw away the fishbone that he
had kept between them as they slept to show to Fionn's seers that they
had not been unfaithful to him.

After many years on the run, Diarmuid's foster father Aengus, distressed at the quarrel, decided to negotiate peace with Fionn, if he was
willing. Fionn was agreeable so Angus went to the High King of Ireland
to seek agreement from him as well. Cormac said that he would grant
him a pardon. Having achieved agreement from the chief of the Fianna
and the High King Aengus, then went to Diarmuid and Gráinne and
asked Diarmuid whether he would also make peace. Diarmuid asserted
that he would, but only under certain conditions. 'What are those conditions?' said Angus. 'The district,' said Diarmuid, 'which my father
had, that is the district of O'Duibhne, Fionn shall not hunt nor chase
therein, and it must be free of rent or tribute to the King of Erin; also
the district of *Benn Damuis*, that is, *Dubhcarn* in Leinster as a gift for
myself from Fionn, for it is the best district in Erin: and also the district
of Kesh Corann in present-day County Sligo from the King of Erin
as dowry for his daughter; and those are the conditions upon which
I would make peace with them.'

Fionn's request for land at Kesh Corann may have stemmed from
the fact that Cormac Mac Airt's maternal grandmother, an O'Dolain
and chief of Corann at that time, lived on the shores of nearby Lough
Fenagh. In any event, a truce was agreed between the protagonists:

And Cormac and Fionn forgave Diarmuid all the harm he had done
as long as he had been outlawed, namely for the space of sixteen
years; and Cormac gave his other daughter for wife and mate to
Fionn, that he might let Diarmuid be, and so they made peace with
each other; and the place that Diarmuid and Gráinne settled in was

Rath Grainne in the district of Kesh Corann in the county of Sligo far
from Fionn and from Cormac.

Rathcormack in County Sligo also lays claim to being the district in
which Diarmuid and Gráinne settled. They point out a ringfort in
the village, named in honour of Cormac[4] – whom it is believed was a
descendant of Diarmuid and Gráinne – and gave the fort and the village
its name. In support of their claim, it can fairly be said that Diarmuid
could not possibly have heard the 'voice of hounds baying' from Kesh
Corann as we shall see later but could easily have done so from where
the village of Rathcormack now stands. Proponents of Kesh Corann as
their home argue that the voices were heard in a dream sequence.

The annals show that following this settlement of the dispute:

Gráinne bore Diarmuid four sons and one daughter; namely,
Donncadh, Eochaidh, Connla, Selbsercach, and Druime; and he
gave the district of Benn Damuis, that is, Dubcarn in Leinster, to his
daughter, and he sent attendants to serve her there. They abode a
long time fulfilling the terms of the peace with each other, and people
used to say that there was not living at the same time with him a man
richer in gold and silver, in kine and cattle-herds and sheep, and who
made more successful raids, than Diarmuid.

This story then should have a happy ending – but it was not to be.

Diarmuid's dreams were disturbed one night by the baying of
hounds. He was startled awake, so that Gráinne caught him and threw
her two arms about him, and asked him what was wrong: 'It is the
voice of hounds baying I have heard,' said Diarmuid, 'and I marvel
to hear it in the night. They are chasing a pig on the slopes of Benn
Gulbain.'

Gráinne was immediately suspicious, as she knew that it was proph-
esised that one day her husband would be killed by the wild boar of
Benn Gulbain (modern-day Benbulben). Fearful that it was a ruse, she
convinced him that whatever he had heard, it was no business of theirs
and they went back to sleep. Shortly Diarmuid was awakened once
again by the sound of hounds in pursuit and could not go back to sleep.

When morning came, he said to his wife: 'I must go to seek the hound whose voice I have heard, since it is day.'

'Do not go, my love,' she said to him.

'I must go,' he replied, 'for I feel a strong compulsion to do so. How can danger arise from such a small affair?'

'Well then,' said Gráinne, 'if you must go, take with thee the *Moralltach*, that is, the sword of Manannán Mac Lir, and the *Gae Derg*.'

'I will not,' said Diarmuid, 'but I will take the *Begalltach* and the *Gae Buidhe* with me and my hound Mac an Cumhall by a chain in my hand.'

When he arrived at Benbulben, Diarmuid found Fionn before him and asked him if it was he that was on the hunt. Fionn replied that it was not he but the men of the Fianna who had come across this wild boar: 'Now it is the wild boar of *Benn Gulban* that the hound has met, and the Fianna do but foolishly in following him; for oftentimes ere now he has escaped them, and thirty warriors of the fian were slain by him this morning. He is even now coming up against the mountain towards us, with the Fianna fleeing before him, and let us leave this hill to him.'

Diarmuid replied that no wild animal would strike fear into his heart, that he would not leave the hill through fear of the boar or any other animal, that he would take him on and slaughter him.

Both men regretted the divisions that had come between them. They could be ambivalent about it but in their hearts they missed the days when they were close friends and comrades in arms, when they enjoyed the thrill of the hunt together.

'You must not hunt this boar,' Fionn replied regretfully, 'for you are under *geasa* (taboo) never to hunt swine, but particularly not this one!'

'Wherefore were those taboos laid upon me?' Diarmuid demanded indignantly.

'That I will tell thee,' said Fionn. He then explained that many years before, when Diarmuid was a boy, his father was asked by his steward Roc Mac Diochmhaire to take his boy, who was Diarmuid's age, in fosterage but he refused: 'It was no long time after that that there arose a quarrel between two of my staghounds about some broken meat that was thrown them,' Fionn continued, 'and the women and the lesser people of the place fled before them, and the others rose to separate them. The son of Roc went between thy father's knees, flying before the staghounds, and he gave the child a mighty, powerful, strong squeeze of his two knees, so that he crushed him to death. Then the steward took the magic wand of Aongus Na Brugh, and with sorcery struck his dead son with that wand so that he made of him a cropped green pig, having neither ears nor tail, and he said: "I conjure thee, my son, that thou have the same length of life as Diarmuid O'Dhuibne, and that it be by thee that he shall fall at last." Then the wild boar rose and stood, and rushed out by the open door. When Aongus heard those spells laid upon thee, he conjured thee never to hunt a swine; and particularly that wild boar that is the wild boar of *Benn Gulban*, and it is not meet for thee to await him upon this hill.'

Diarmuid then became suspicious that Fionn had never fully forgiven him, and that he had been lured by treachery to his death on this mountainside. Nevertheless, he was confident that taboo or no taboo he would – he must – take a stand and by the power of his arms kill the enchanted boar and overcome the curse. 'By my word,' said Diarmuid, 'it is to slay me that thou hast made this hunt, O Fionn, and if it be here I am fated to die, I have no power now to shun it.'

As the words were spoken, the wild boar came up the face of the mountain with the Fianna after it. When Diarmuid saw the size and power of the huge animal, he regretted not taking Gráinne's advice: 'Woe to him that heeds not the counsel of a good wife, for Gráinne bade me at early morn today take with me the *Moralltach* and the *Gae Derg*.'

As the pig rushed towards him, he made a careful cast with the sword he carried but, breaking it in two, it had no effect whatsoever on the beast. Then the wild boar made a savage leap at Diarmuid, tripping him. Diarmuid rose from the ground and vaulted on to the beast's back, the better to strike a fatal blow on him. The boar twisted, Diarmuid landed back to front and the boar fled down the hill, trying to shake Diarmuid off.

After that he fled away until he reached *Easa Ruadh* (the Red Waterfall) of *Mac Badhairn* in *Béal Atha Seanaigh* in County Donegal and having reached the red stream he gave three nimble leaps across the fall hither and thither, yet he could not shake off Diarmuid in all that time; and he came back by the same path until be reached up to the height of the mountain again. And when he had reached the top he threw Diarmuid off his back; and when he was fallen to the earth the wild boar made an eager exceeding mighty spring upon him, and ripped out his bowels and his entrails so that they fell about his legs. Howbeit, as the boar was leaving the hill, Diarmuid made a triumphant cast of the hilt of the sword that chanced to be still in his hand, so that he dashed out the boar's brains and left him dead on the ground.

(P.W. Joyce, *Ancient Celtic Romances*)

Fionn and the Fianna had watched the mighty struggle and Fionn now came up to where Diarmuid lay dying on the ground. Although Fionn did his best to forgive Diarmuid for having wronged him, deep in his heart there was no forgiveness, but still only jealousy and now it spilled out: 'It likes me well to see thee in that plight, O Diarmuid,' said he; 'and I grieve that all the women of Erin are not now gazing upon thee: for thy excellent beauty is turned to ugliness, and thy choice form to deformity.'

'Nevertheless, it is in thy power to heal me, O Fionn,' said Diarmuid, 'if it were thy pleasure to do so.'

'How should I heal thee?' said Fionn, pretending not to know. 'Easily,' replied Diarmuid; 'for when thou didst get the noble precious gift of divining at the Boyne, it was granted thee that to whomsoever thou

should give a drink from the palms of thy hands, he should after that be young, fresh, and sound from any sickness he might have at that time.'

'I know no well whatever upon this mountain,' said Fionn.

'That is not true,' said Diarmuid, 'for but nine paces from thee is the best well of pure water in the world.'

Fionn went to the well and, cupping his hands, lifted the water. Turning, he went to carry it to Diarmuid, but his heart wasn't in it and as he walked he let the water trickle through his fingers. When he told Diarmuid that it was impossible to carry water this way, Diarmuid replied sadly: 'I see that of thine own will, thou didst let it from thee.'

Fionn then went for the water a second time, but as he returned to the dying man, his mind turned to Gráinne and how she was taken from him. His heart filled with anger and once again he allowed the water to leak to the ground, saying that it was impossible to bring water in this way. 'Not so, Fionn,' said Diarmuid in anguish, 'I have killed the boar for you, why now will you let me die?'

At this, Oscar stepped forward from the assembled Fianna, none of whom wished for Diarmuid to die, and swore an oath: 'I swear upon my arms,' said Oscar, 'that if thou bring not the water speedily, O Fionn, there shall not leave this hill but either thou or I!'

Fearful of the threat that Oscar had made, Fionn returned to the well for a third time. It was too late: as he came up with the water, Diarmuid's head fell back and he was dead. His friend Oscar covered him with his cloak and all the Fianna present raised three loud shouts of sorrow for their dead comrade. 'I swear,' said Oscar, 'had I known that it was with intent to kill Diarmuid that thou madest the hunt of *Benn Gulban*, that thou wouldst never have made it. Better you had died than our champion!'

Gráinne sat that day on the highest rampart of *Rath Gráinne*, watching for Diarmuid's return. When at last the Fianna came into view and she saw Diarmuid's dog being led by Fionn, she realised what had happened, fainted and fell off the rampart. When she opened her eyes and was given the news, she and her women and all of the people of her court raised three loud bitter cries of lamentation, 'which were heard in the glens and wildernesses around and which pierced the clouds of heaven'.

Versions differ as to Gráinne's subsequent actions. In some, Aengus takes Diarmuid's body to his home at *Brú na Bóinne*. In others, Gráinne swears her children to avenge their father's death upon Fionn, while further versions claim that she grieves until she dies herself. In other versions she is reconciled with Fionn, negotiates peace between him and her sons and marries him as was originally intended. Thus ends the story of the most famous lovers of our mythological past and whose 'beds' are to be found all over Ireland. Did such a warrior band ever exist? Could such a marvellous chain of events ever have happened? I believe it did and could, as there is always an element of truth in these old legends that have been handed down to us over the centuries.

Should you doubt the truth of the story, you may go to the slopes of Benbulben, where even yet the water gushes forth from the well that could have saved Diarmuid's life. Or you may go to the Gleniff Horseshoe in North Sligo where, high on the mountainside, you will see Diarmuid and Gráinne's cave, where long ago they hid on a bed of sea sand in dread of the wrath of Fionn Mac Cumhaill.

5

QUEEN MAEVE: IRELAND'S FIRST FEMINIST?

No narrative of Sligo would be complete without a mention of Maeve, warrior Queen of Connacht, and her resting place atop Knocknarea known as *Miosgán Meadhbha* (Maeve's Cairn). Maeve's Cairn is located at the summit of Knocknarea Mountain which, at 1,014 feet, dominates the landscape to the west of Sligo. The cairn measures some 180 feet across and over 30 feet high, making it the largest such tomb in Ireland outside the Boyne Valley. Its shape and structure (and the results of archaeology in the area) have led to the tomb being classified as a Neolithic passage tomb. It is estimated that the stones used in the construction weigh approximately 44,000 tons.

Here, as befitting Iron Age royalty, the Queen is said to have been buried upright, facing the ancient enemy in Ulster. No excavation has ever taken place on the site, so there is no archaeological evidence to support this, nor do we need it. Until it is proven otherwise, we may safely say she is. Let her rest in peace as her spirit gazes out over the countryside, imbuing our imagination with great and daring deeds of long ago. Earthbound, we gaze in awe at her cairn atop the mountain, a fitting tribute to the legends and her reign; it has stood the test of time and inspires yet poets and people alike.

The poet W.B. Yeats wrote:

> …The wind has bundled up the clouds high over Knock-na-rea,
> And thrown the thunder on the stones for all that Maeve can say.

Angers that are like noisy clouds have set our hearts abeat;
But we have all bent low and low and kissed the quiet feet
Of Cathleen, the daughter of Houlihan ...

That may be so but surely we can be forgiven if we, her romantic admir-
ers, believe that it is she who commands the clouds and thunder and
revels in these celestial displays.

It was through the Middletons, his uncle's people, that Yeats first
got his interest in the stories of the countryside. In *Reveries over
Childhood and Youth*, he wrote that 'The first fairy stories I heard
were in the cottages about their houses ...' (in Rosses Point). He was
much influenced by the visions of his Uncle George Pollexfen's maid,
Mary Battle, too. From a window in Rosses Point, she saw Queen
Maeve and her warriors, 'fine and dashing looking,'[5] riding towards
her from Maeve's Cairn atop the mountain. Had it not been for Mary
Battle, these lines from 'The Hosting of the Sidhe' might never have
been written:

The host is riding from Knocknarea
And over the grave of Clooth-na-bare;
Caolte tossing his burning hair
And Niamh calling 'Away, come away:
Empty your heart of its mortal dream.
The winds awaken, the leaves whirl round,
Our cheeks are pale, our hair is unbound,
Our breasts are heaving, our eyes a-gleam,
Our arms are waving, our lips are apart;
And if any gaze on our rushing band,
We come between him and the deed of his hand,
We come between him and the hope of his heart.'
The host is rushing 'twixt night and day,
And where is there hope or deed as fair?
Caolte tossing his burning hair,
And Niamh calling 'Away, come away.'

Was Queen Maeve Ireland's first feminist?

She and her husband King Ailill lived in the first century AD. Renowned in history and legend as a warrior of Amazonian proportions, Maeve is rivalled only by Granuaile or Boudica, Queen of the British Celts, for her fierce reputation. She is best remembered for her part in the epic story in the 'Ulster Cycle' of the *Táin Bó Cúailnge*, commonly known as 'The Cattle Raid of Cooley'.

Engaged in a fierce debate with her husband over which of them had brought the most treasure, property and possessions into their marriage, she commanded all their wealth and assets to be brought before them. Maeve matched, cow for cow, horse for horse and jewel for jewel everything that her husband owned – except for Ailill's magnificent bull called the *Finnbheannach* (white horned), for which his wife had no equal in her herd.

Maeve was disappointed but equally determined that no man was going to get the better of her. Word came back to her eventually that in Cooley, County Louth in the province of Ulster, there was a bull in the possession of a farmer there that was as good as, or better than, her husband's.

Messengers were sent out to secure the bull, called the *Donn Cuailgne*, for Maeve, but she was refused. The armies of Connacht were immediately assembled to march on Ulster. Despite a valiant defence by the Ulster champion, Cúchulainn, the bull was captured and brought to Maeve.

This should have been the end of the matter, but it wasn't. Ailill's bull, resenting the competition, charged the *Donn Cuailgne*. A fierce fight ensued, which ended with the Brown Bull of Cooley passing through Maeve's royal seat at Cruachain, carrying the mangled carcass of Ailill's bull on its horns. On returning to his Ulster homeland, 'the heart burst within the great bull of Cooley and it expired.'

The ancient storytellers leave no clue as to what effect this debacle had on the peace and tranquillity of the royal household.

6

THE ENCHANTED CAVE
OF KESH CORANN

The Hill of Kesh Corann in South County Sligo, with its associated caves, has long been connected with magic, mystery and myth. The caves are said to be connected to other caverns at Cruachan in the county of Roscommon, some 25 miles distant, known as 'the Hellmouth of Ireland'. Gabriel Beranger in his diary, written in 1779, wrote:

> … a woman in the county of Roscommon having an unruly calf could never get him home unless driving him by holding him by the tail; that one day he tried to escape and dragged the woman, against her will into the Hellmouth door; that unable to stop him, she ran after him without quitting her hold, and continued running until next morning. She came out at Kishcorren, to her own amazement and that of the neighbouring people.

The Hellmouth door is also known as Oweynagat (Cave of the Cats) and may still be seen to this day near the village of Tulsk, County Roscommon. The name Oweynagat is thought to come from the magical wildcats featured in 'Bricriu's Feast' that once emerged from the cave to attack three Ulster warriors before being tamed by Cúchulainn.

The caves were excavated 1929-30 and were found to contain the bones of the European brown bear, giant elk, ox, reindeer, red deer, Arctic lemming, horse, ass, sheep, dog, goat and pig, some from the Mesolithic, Neolithic and Bronze ages (8000 to 600 BC). Only scant human remains were found, but given its enchanted reputation, perhaps this is not surprising. It is possible that human and animal teeth may have been placed in the caves as part of ritual activities associated with the Festival of Lughnasa. One of the caves beside the one known as Cormac's was used as a hedge school during Penal times, when learning and the Catholic religion were forbidden in Ireland. Given its vantage point, it was a good choice as soldiers, spies or other unwelcome visitors could be spotted a long way off.

According to Marion O'Dowd in an article in *Dedicated to Sligo*, the Lughnasa assembly at the base of the mountain was the largest in County Sligo, dating to the ninth century but with possible pre-Christian origins. Also known as Garland Sunday and celebrated on the last Sunday in July, people travelled from all parts of the county for a day of reunion, music, dancing and faction fighting: 'Tradition stated that the assembly began when a fiddler led the people up the mountain to the caves.'

Garland Sunday is still celebrated in the area, with numerous games and competitions, including a 'King of the Hill' event, turf footing and hay rope making, concluding with a social and waltzing competition in the White Hall, Keash.

Three lakes in the area are named after three sisters: Cé, who lived in a magical lake under the Hill of Keash; Léib, who lived in Lough Labe (*Loch na Léibe*), and Carabhac, at Lough Arrow (*Loch Arabhac*). They were daughters of the sea deity Manannán Mac Lir of the *Tuatha De Danaan*.

The mountain is reputed to have come into being as a result of Deirdre, of the magical race of the *Tuatha De Danaan*, being transformed into a sow when she ate enchanted acorns. The sow, known as Cael Ceis, maddened by her fate, ran amok through the countryside, causing death and destruction. Many tried time and again to kill the pig without success until Corann, harper to the *De Danaan* God Dian Cécht, lulled the demonic pig to sleep with his skilful playing of the harp so that the hunters could kill it. The mountain itself is said to have been formed from the carcase of the sleeping sow. As a reward, Corann was given the large tract of land that encased the giant sow.

Another of the legends of the mountain tells us of a great hunt organised by Finn of the Fianna. While the hunt was in progress, Finn went to the top of Kesh Corann with his friend Conan and his dogs Bran and Sceolan. Standing on the Brú or 'Hunting Mound', they watched the

Fianna hunt deer, wolf and fowl through the countryside underneath: Corann, Tirerril and Leyney.

A chief called Conoran Mac Imeadal, King of the *Sidhe* of Kesh Corann, was overlord of the area at that time. Conaran's people were the descendants of the *Tuatha De Danaan*, who still carried resentment for their defeat at the hands of the Milesians, from whom Finn was descended. Conaran could see Finn, but Finn could not see him. The fairy race remains invisible to mortals unless they wish to reveal themselves to us. When he heard the shouting and baying of hounds, he was extremely annoyed that the Fianna were hunting there without extending the courtesy of asking his permission. Hatching a plan for revenge, he sent three of his daughters, Caevóg, Iaran and Cuillean Ceann Rua (Cuillean the Redhead), to the opening of one of the caves. Sitting down there, they put three enchanted hanks of yarn on crooked holly sticks and began to reel them off.

Finn and Conan spotted them and came closer to investigate. What they saw was three ugly old hags at their work. In Lady Gregory's *Gods and Fighting Men* they are described as having 'their coarse hair tossed, their eyes red and bleary, their teeth sharp and crooked, their arms very long, their nails like the tips of cow's horns, and the three spindles in their hands.' Additionally they had 'long scraggy necks that could turn all the way around, similar to that of a chicken. Their bodies were covered with a bristle of hair and fur and fluff, they had moustaches poking under their noses, woolly wads grew out of their ears.'

Conan, suspicious of the three women who had so mysteriously appeared, urged Finn to ignore them and continue on their way. Finn, replying that the Fianna feared nothing, strode resolutely into the cave. Conan, having no choice but to follow his leader and unaware that it was enchantment they were spinning, passed through the hanks of yarn to get a better look at the women. Immediately the men became weak and their limbs began to tremble. This is the effect the hags desired and so they immediately took hold of the men and tied them up securely. Two other members of the Fianna went through the spindles to rescue their friends and they too became weak and were caught in the same way. Caoilte and several other members of the Fianna rushed to help and, passing the spindles, also fell victim. All were dragged into the cave. At the cave entrance the hounds, being too wise to follow, set up a great cry for their masters,

who had left them. Heaps of game – deer, wild pigs hares and badgers
that the hunters had caught – were stacked in heaps outside.

According to legend, the three women picked up swords to put an
end to the men they had captured. Before commencing the slaughter,
they looked outside to see if there were any more of the Fianna left to
capture and they spotted a tall man striding towards them. It was Goll
Mac Morna, known as the 'Flame of Battle'. The women had taken the
spindles in but as it was three against one, they felt confident in chal-
lenging Goll anyway. The four of them engaged in a fierce struggle until,
with one fierce blow, Goll beheaded two of the witches. Overcoming the
remaining woman, Caevog, he tied her up with the straps of his shield.
Raising the sword over his head to decapitate her as well, she cried out:
'O champion that was never worsted, strong man that never was beaten,
I put my life under your protection. Is it not better for you to get Finn
and the Fianna safe and whole than to have my blood. I swear by the
Gods my people swear by, I will give them back to you again.'

With that, Goll set her free and they went together into the cave, where
Finn and the Fianna were lying in a heap on the floor. Goll demanded of
her that she would release all of them, which she did forthwith: 'Finn and
Fergus, Oisin and the twenty nine sons of Morna and all the rest'.

Immediately Conaran's fourth daughter, Iamach, springing out of
nowhere and fierce at the killing of her sisters, launched an attack on
the Fianna. She too, ferocious and powerful though she was, was slain
after a fierce battle with Goll.

Of Conoran, who caused all the trouble in the first place, history or
legend tells us nothing. The Fianna, amazed and delighted with the turn
of events, made no delay but leaving the cave, went down the hillside
to continue their hunting. Understandably there was great rejoicing at
their escape and in the following days Oisin wrote a poem in praise of
the great warrior, Goll, who saved their lives.

Replete with myths and legends of former times, Kesh Corann of the
Bricklieves, with its extraordinary caves and outline, ranks among the
great mountains of Sligo, vying for prominence with Benbulben and
Knocknarea. Surrounded with an aura of romance and charm, it speaks to
us of its former greatness and is still a popular place for visitors who wish
to immerse themselves in the landscape and explore its mysteries.

7

Strange Occurrences

Ballisodare Mills

In the village of Ballisodare, overlooking the waterfall, there stands the ruins of a church built by St Fechin in the seventh century. A man called Culbertson (followed by Middleton and Pollexfen), operated the most comprehensive milling enterprise anywhere in Ireland at this place. It was a thriving business well into the late years of the twentieth century. The extensive operation had its modest origins when St Fechin established the mill as part of the monastic settlement in his time.

The mill burned down in 1856. The explanation of how it happened is an interesting one: In many parts of Ireland it was the custom to ritually 'bleed' a small farm animal in honour of St Martin's feast day on 11 November. It was believed that Martin was martyred by being thrown into a millstream and killed by the wheel and because of this no wheel, whether millwheel, spinning wheel or cartwheel was allowed to turn on his feast day. St Martin was very unforgiving if the prohibition was not observed and many were the stories told of the saint's retribution.

Workmen at the Ballisodare mill, wishing to honour the prohibition and fearful of the consequences, would not work on the saint's day. Management, however, insisted that the mill operate as usual. The dispute escalated and on the afternoon of St Martin's Day 1856, the mill caught fire in mysterious circumstances. Nine workmen were burned to death or died jumping from the building; major damage was done to the fabric of the mill and the contents destroyed. Following the disaster, the owner fell into bad health and died some years later.

In the succeeding years the mill was brought back into production, but was closed for work on each feast of St Martin until the outbreak of war in 1939. The mill is no longer in use and, like St Fechin's church, stood until recent times as a monument and reminder of Ballisodare's commercial and monastic past. During Ireland's 'Celtic Tiger' era, the mill was torn down and modern apartments built in its place.

BANSHEE (*BEAN SIDHE*)

The banshee, from the Irish *bean sidhe,* meaning literally 'fairy woman', is a supernatural female being. She is seen as a death messenger from the underworld, predicting the demise of a neighbour or family member. The belief is widespread throughout Ireland. She is held to be an unearthly attendant specifically attached to the ancient families of Ireland, the true descendants of the Gaelic race, those who have Mac and Ó as part of their names, for:

> By Mac and Ó
> You'll always know
> True Irishmen they say.
> But if they lack
> The Ó and Mac,
> No Irishmen are they.

The belief is asserted in James Clarence Mangan's *A Lamentation for the Death of Sir Maurice Fitzgerald.* Fitzgerald was killed in action in Flanders in 1642:

> From Loughmoe to yellow Dunanore
> There was fear; the traders of Tralee
> Gathered up their golden store,
> And prepared to flee;

For, in ship and hall from night till morning,
Showed the first faint beamings of the sun,
All the foreigners heard the warning
Of the Dreaded One!

'This,' they spake, 'portendeth death to us,
If we fly not swiftly from our fate!
Self-conceited idiots! Thus
Ravingly to prate!
Not for base-born higgling Saxon trucksters
Ring laments like those by shore and sea!
Not for churls with souls like hucksters
Waileth our Banshee!

For the high Milesian race alone
Ever flows the music of her woe!
For slain heir to bygone throne,
And for Chief laid low!
Hark! ... Again, methinks, I hear her weeping
Yonder! Is she near me now, as then?
Or was but the night-wind sweeping
Down the hollow glen?

Although in the case of Fitzgerald the Mac and Ó does not appear as a prefix they were a thoroughly Hibernicised family who claimed to be descended from the territorial Goddess Áine. Many families under pressure to adopt English ways, or who just wished to do so, dropped the prefix Mac or Ó. For instance, Sweeney would have been *Mac Suibhne* originally and Rourke would have been known as *Ó'Ruairc* – the banshee knows the difference! Conversely the banshee does not cry for all Gaelic families, nor indeed for all members of the same family.

Illustrative of the importance of the banshee to families is the story of two chieftains comparing their assets. When cattle, land and gold were taken into account, their wealth was found to be equal. No matter how they tried, one could not best the other. Finally one of the disputants, the O'Connor Sligo, played his trump card: 'Ah, but the banshee

follows our family,' he declared triumphantly, demonstrating how much prestige was attached to the tradition.

The cry of the banshee is like the *caoin* of the keeners of long ago: local women who gathered to cry or 'keen' at wakes. Lady Gregory described it as 'rising to a high pitch and then falling down again', receding and rising. She is seldom seen and when she is, it can be in the form of a bird or a woman dressed in white, combing her long hair. The warning can also come in the form of three knocks, even on the window of a high-rise building in cities.

'I heard the banshee meself,' a Grange woman, formerly of Largydonnell, told me once.

The Master [Martin Bernard Mc Gowan] was on the run. They're crying, me father says, the Master must be shot. Me father had a nerve like a horse but the sound shook him. He thought it might be Dotty and Nora crying on the Masters street. Hugh, the Masters brother, heard a noise in the byre and went out to the byres to look at the cows, everything was calm. He heard nothing. It was the banshee that was crying. He [Hugh] was dead and buried in a week's time, he had meningitis. It was for Hugh he was crying. The cry sounded like two girls wailing – a mournful cry.

The thing about it is that the family that the banshee cries for never hears the banshee at all. It was the Cornyns that heard the banshee. I remember it, Joe, if you heard the Banshee once you'd remember her.

My neighbour, Bernie Kelly, described for me his vivid recollections of experiences he had with the banshee. The first one concerned a next-door neighbour: 'The cries away out down the fields the night Bartley Gillen died was fierce. They heard it way over in the Coastwatching hut too. Brigid got him dead in the bed in the morning.'

He had a similar experience when another neighbour – and relation – passed away:

I heard it the day before James Donlevy there below died too. He was an uncle of me mothers. A grand night it was. We were young going to school. The kitchen bed was here and the whole lot of us gathered round the fire, Dan and me and all. James McGowan, yer granduncle, God be good to him, was here too, he used to help us out with the work and come down rambling at night as well. When James'd be going home me father used to go out to the road with him. He was out talking to James on the road before they parted. He'd go round then to check the cows, all he had was an oul' candle, there was no flashlights like now. We were here round the fire an' the front door was open, don't be talking, the crying started. The lonesomest wailing ever ye heard. We thought it was me mother was crying outside, she had gone out to see what was keeping me father. I jumped into the bed here an' Maggie too. It was wicked with the crying an isn't it ashow to God me mother or father never heard it. Poor Mary Clinton heard it because she was telling me mother the next day.

In me grandmother's time they used to make butter an' sell it at a market in Kinlough that was held on certain day in the week. Me father's father an' mother was away at market. My uncle Pat, my aunt Maria as well as my father John were here, young ones at the time. That night they heard the banshee way there below in the plot crying away. They were afraid of their life. A grand evening or night it was and the crying was up and down and back and forth. Not a hate on him an' he was got dead in bed the next morning, me father's father, Dan Kelly was his name.

Should we believe in the banshee? Does such a creature really exist, or is it a product merely of a more credulous past?

Dr Patricia Lysaght of the Department of Irish Folklore at University College Dublin gave a lecture to Sligo Field Club some years ago to a packed audience. It was an interesting and well-informed lecture, as she expounded on folk views of the banshee as a 'death messenger', its connection with families, its aural and visual manifestations and much more. Presenting the case for and against the banshee she explored whether it was a figment of the imagination, perhaps triggered by some animal cry when a death in the locality was expected.

Critically analysing the phenomenon, she seemed to me unconvinced of the banshee's existence. Following the lecture, comments were invited from the audience. The number of people who stood up, one after another, to tell stories of their personal encounters with the death messenger, too many to relate here, was quite amazing. Could so many people be wrong? I don't think so, and the experience proved, to me at least, that the banshee is alive and well in Sligo.

THE DEATH COACH

Also known as the 'headless coach' or *'cóiste bodhar'*, this is a spectral horse-drawn carriage that careens along the roads at night to foretell a death or carry the unwary passenger to its lair. Once it has come to Earth it can never return empty. Thus, once the death of an individual has been decided by a greater power, mortals may do nothing to prevent it.

This is the story of the Death Coach as I recall hearing it from my mother. The incident happened somewhere between Sligo town and Bunduff:

> Beware the Death Coach, *agradh*. When you see it, someone is going to die. And if yer not careful, they can take you away. Me mother often told me a story about when she was a wee girl; she was coming home from Sligo town with her mother, that would be my grandmother. Y'know people walked to town in their bare feet then. Shoes wasn't as plentiful as they are now.

It came late at night on them; they were tired from walking along
the road when they heard the sound of a carriage coming behind
them. Me grandmother was delighted to get a lift when it stopped
and the door opened. She took my mother's hand and was about
to get into the coach when she noticed that the driver had no head.
She got such a fright that she grabbed the child, turned around and
got away from there as quick as she could. Me mother often told
me about it and about her mother wondering what would have happened if they had got in.

There is a widespread belief in Northern Europe in the Wild Hunt,
which is a group of ghostly hunters riding along the sky at night, on the
sea or on lonely roads. They are often seen headless or with their skulls
under their arms. There is only one instance of this that I know of and
it happened to Mullaghmore fishermen, who were out at sea fishing
herring at Bomore Island. They saw a death coach coming towards them
along the water from the direction of Slieve League in County Donegal
and heading southwards. They blessed themselves and as it was passing
by, one man plucked up courage and shouted: 'From whence to where?'
The reply came back: 'From hell to Palmerston's funeral.'

8

GHOSTS

HAUNTED HOUSES

The ruined castles of Ireland speak of a battle-scarred past. Many of them, where they exist at all, are occupied now by phantoms of a class of people who once held the power of life and death over those who served under them. 'Speaking monuments of the troubled and insecure state of the country' was how George Burrow, author of *Lavengro*, described them.

The changing tides of history and fortune forced the once-powerful landed gentry to abandon their palatial holdings. Their ghosts and the ghosts of their retainers clung, however, and often remained in the crumbling 'big houses' and deserted mansions. Behind the vacant windows and lifeless walls, troubled shadows sometimes flit; a palpable air of mystery and menace remains. 'Beyond here be dragons', the ancient map makers inscribed across the frontiers of the uncharted world. 'Across the villages of fishermen and turners of the earth,' Yeats once wrote, 'so different are these from us, we can write but one line that is certain: "Here are ghosts."'

The air of Ireland is full of restless spirits because of our war-torn history, McIlhenny claimed in Seamus Deane's book, *Reading in the Dark*: Lord Leitrim, the wicked landlord of Ramelton, County Donegal, who was shot dead because of his policy of rack-renting and evictions, continued to travel the road on which he met his maker every night. The horse and rider, silhouetted against the night sky, made no noise:

It [the figure] galloped along until it neared the spot in the hedge, and then, for a second or two, you could hear its hoofbeats drumming. As you heard these, the figure on the horse vanished for an instant; then when you looked up the road, there it was again, gliding away into the darkness in absolute silence.

Lord Leitrim and his kind, McIlhinney believed, would be like that until the day of judgement: never alive, never dead, just shadows in the air.

Tom William Higgins, one of Lord Palmerston's bailiffs, lived in Cliffoney village, North Sligo. His was a reign of terror, as he impounded cattle for late rent payments or, at the head of the infamous 'crowbar brigade', tore down the homes of tenants who were unable to pay. Higgins was one day collecting rents in the village of Cliffoney. He came to the house until recently occupied by Patsy Harrison, to collect the rent from the tenant farmer that lived there at the time. This poor man was a halfpenny short of the full amount of his rent and, desperate to stay out of trouble, went to a neighbour for a loan. Neighbours recall that when he returned, he found that the agent and his men had already knocked down his house with crowbars, but:

> Death lays his icy hand on kings:
> Sceptre and Crown
> Must tumble down,
> And in the dust be equal made
> With the poor crookèd scythe and spade …

When Higgins' turn came to meet his maker, neighbours were alarmed, but not surprised, when they heard 'terrible noises' in the house every night following his demise.

In addition to the noises, locals witnessed the bizarre sight of a 'rat wearing glasses' seen skulking around the walls of the house. The story seems so bizarre and unbelievable as to bring a smile. It must be a joke! Surely such a spectre could only be the figment of overactive imaginations. However, when unrelated witnesses insist on its truth and tell you that Higgins wore glasses when he was alive, you know it's no jest.

The Bible tells us of demons expelled from the human body entering that of a pig – and perhaps there's poetic justice in the image: a rat in life condemned to live out eternity in a rat's body.

The house was later bought by a family and, disturbed by the upheaval, they sent for the parish priest. An exorcism was performed, which brought an end to the haunting. Afterwards, a sealed upstairs room was all that remained as evidence that some unnatural phenomenon had occurred there at one time.

Only a few stones remain now as mute reminders of the house that once held so much power. Beside it can still be seen the cattle pound, where the cattle of impoverished tenants were once seized and held for non-payment of rent.

LISHEEN HOUSE

The ruins of Lisheen House stand on the outskirts of Strandhill, County Sligo, overlooking the splendid Ballisodare Bay. The original building was constructed in 1798 by William Phibbs, an Anglo-Irish landlord. His grandson (also named William), who acquired several thousand acres in the Coolera area during the Cromwellian confiscations, was a man of considerable wealth and property. In 1840, he decided to build a new palatial twenty-three room mansion in the townland of Lisheen (meaning 'the little fort' or *lios*) that would reflect the family's opulence and importance. The full place name, *Lisheenacooravan*, means 'the little fort on the white level plain'.

Owen Phibbs, an archaeologist and son of William (the builder of the house), crammed the house with ancient treasures from the Far East, Syria, and Egypt. The objects were housed in a long gallery on the first floor, which became known as 'The Museum'. Trouble started soon afterwards, when the mansion became infested with a particularly unpleasant and malicious poltergeist. A strange figure was often seen on the stairway at night, accompanied soon afterwards by terrible loud crashes heard throughout the house. Broken pottery and curios would be found on the floor the next morning. On one occasion the whole house shook violently – all in the house fled in terror. After this event, servants refused to stay inside the house. Shortly afterwards, a gardener was terrified by a tall, dark, shadowy figure seen disappearing into the sea, laughing maniacally. The gardener was also said to have fled in terror, never to return.

Is there anything in the past of Lisheen to which we can point as a source of its unquiet spirits?

William Phibbs' reputation as a landlord was poor. Vain and arrogant, he demanded that tenants salute him as he drove by in his carriage. Charging exorbitant rents for the meagre dwellings and plots of land on which these tenants lived, Phibbbs was quick to evict entire families when they could no longer pay. Needless to say, many of those who found themselves on the side of the road died. The stones from their demolished homesteads were used to build the boundary fences and demesne walls of Lisheen that can still be seen today.

In the 1900s, the house was handed over to a group of Jesuit priests, who performed Mass daily for some weeks in an attempt to exorcise the poltergeist. Unfortunately, this failed and they also fled the property. Unable to rid the house of its infestation, D.W. Phibbs sold it in 1940.

Having no feeling for the poor, it is not surprising to learn that a curse, the 'widow's curse', was placed on the house and family. As the story goes, a widow who had been pushed to the brink of ruin laid a curse upon Lisheen and those who dwelt there. The day would come, she said, when the birds of the air would build their nests in the ruins of Lisheen Castle and she condemned the family to walk the castle for all time; their ghosts and the ghosts of their children would haunt the ruins for eternity.

And so it has come to pass. Although denied by surviving family members, the house is reputed to be haunted by old Phibbs' coach and horses. They glide noiselessly up the avenue at midnight, halt briefly at the main door and disappear as silently as they came. Crows and magpies fly in and out of the desolate, ivy-covered ruin that is now Lisheen, their raucous quarrelling disturbing the countryside. Contrary to its opulent and extravagant past, the walls stand now as a foreboding blot on the landscape, reminding us of how transient are the conceits of man.

DANNY CUMMINS

Ramblers went on foot to their destinations along the darkened roads of long ago. Haunted houses, encounters with banshees, headless death coaches, ghosts of the departed and nocturnal apparitions of frightening black dogs were commonplace. Around the winter fires where these stories were told, there were few who had not a tale to recount of a strange or frightening encounter with things that were not a part of the human world, stories such as that of Danny Cummins.

Danny and two brothers, James and Frank Donlevy, were walking home from Cliffoney village late at night. About a mile from home, near the end of the Burra Road, they saw 'this figure up agin the ditch, lying across the wall'. There was nothing unusual about individuals making their way on foot from one place, or house, to another along the darkened roads of Ireland at that time.

Danny shouted out a friendly greeting to the stranger: 'Me bully fella, why don't you come away with us,' he said. They were all young men in high good spirits, afraid of nothing, kings of their world.

At Donlevy's house, the friends parted. Here Danny had to make his way home alone across the fields. He didn't know it at that moment, but his life was shortly to change forever. As he made his way across the fields, a shadowy creature came before him and launched a savage attack. Defending himself as best he could, he was no match for the ferocious onslaught. The apparition 'kicked him and rowlt him', across the fields until he was put crashing through Anthony Rogers' door. He did not know or recognise the person or thing he fought; later he could not say for sure if it was man or demon. Exhausted and badly shaken from the encounter, he was unable to leave Rogers' until morning. Neighbours said he was never the same man again. Emigrating to America shortly afterwards, with his wife, he was never heard from again.

When word of the affray went out through the village, many speculated that the spectre was a landlord's agent who had died some time before, with whom Cummins had a disagreement. The man often rambled at Anthony Rogers', an ill-reputed house and favourite meeting place for those associated with Lord Palmerston's lodges. 'Poor fella,'

Bernie Kelly recalled, 'My father remembered when he went away, the crickets left his house and came over here. They were still here when I was a-growing up.'

JOHN FEENEY

John Feeney of Aughagad was born in 1827. When he was an old man, he told his son Michael about a ghostly encounter that happened during Penal times in Ireland. The story began with a fierce fight between McMorrough of Drumcliffe and a landlord's bailiff. The bailiff was on horseback and armed with a sword. McMorrough had only a blackthorn stick with which to defend himself. He was losing the fight when, in a last desperate bid, he threw the stick, knocking the man off the horse. The agent died in the fall, but before he passed to the next world, he vowed that vengeance would be his: 'Dead or alive, I will have my revenge on you,' he swore.

Forced to leave home and go on the run, McMorrough became a hunted man. Yeomen scoured the countryside, seeking to avenge the death. McMurrough was forced to live the life of a fugitive, sleeping in 'safe houses' and moving about only at night. A year or so later, when his nocturnal wanderings took him past Drumcliffe cemetery at the dead hour, Feeney

recalled that the vengeful spirit appeared before McMorrough, 'riding on the same horse he rode at the fight and dressed in the same way'. Seizing the reins of the mule that McMurrough rode, the demented shade attempted to force him through the cemetery gate. A desperate struggle followed. Several times, the dead man almost succeeded in forcing McMorrough through and each time he struggled free. Blow for blow, the fierce contest carried on through the night until dawn streaked the weary sky and the loud call of a cock from a neighbouring farm shrilled across fields and churchyard:

> I have heard,
> The cock that is the trumpet to the morn,
> Doth with his lofty and shrill-sounding throat
> Awake the God of day, and at his warning,
> Whether in sea or fire, in earth or air
> The extravagant spirit hies
> To his confine …

> - Horatio to Marcellus in *Hamlet*

Ceasing the struggle at once, the ghostly horse and rider melted with a despairing cry into the deep shadows that lurched across the slanting headstones in the graveyard. McMurrough fell exhausted; the cock's call had saved him, but he never again ventured to pass Drumcliffe churchyard by day or night.

JAMES McGOVERN

James McGovern and his wife lived long ago in a mud hut beside 'Big' John Callery's at the end of the 'Green Road' in Mullaghmore, County Sligo. Following a long illness, James lay dying. Two neighbours went to visit and offer help to his wife. On their way to the house, near Pat Charlie's, they were surprised to meet the sick man on the road; it was a moonlit night, so his features were clearly visible. However, they thought it strange when he passed by without responding to their greeting.

Pleased to see that he had recovered, they decided to continue to the house anyway. On arriving, they were astonished to discover that James had passed away shortly before. The remains lay before them on what had been his sickbed.

Following the wake and funeral, James' wife lived on her own. As time went on, neighbours' visits became less frequent, so she was delighted one night to hear a knock on the door. Opening it, she froze in terror at the sight of her dead husband standing there. She stood for an instant and, not knowing what else to do, slammed the door shut. A few nights later, the same thing happened again. This time she went to Father Malachai Brennan in nearby Cliffoney to have her husband prayed for and to ask the priest what she should do. He advised her to keep a bottle of holy water on the dresser. When the spirit returned, she should invite him in and ask if there was any way she could help him.

A few days later, the knock came to the door again but this time, even though she was deadly afraid, she was prepared. Knowing the holy water was in the house, she felt secure. When she opened the door, there was her dead husband again. This time it was different, though: he looked disturbed. She addressed him anyway, as the priest had advised:

'James,' she said, 'won't you come in?'

'How can I come in,' he responded angrily, 'when you have holy water in the house?'

Losing her courage, the woman slammed the door, shutting out the terrifying vision. The appearances became a regular occurrence. Eventually the distracted woman could take it no longer and moved to the neighbouring townland of Carnduff. She was aghast when the visits continued there. According to Annie C----, who remembered the events, she never did any good after that. Even though the neighbours were kind and sympathetic to the troubled woman, there was nothing they could do.

The story does not have a happy ending: James' widow could not placate his tormented spirit or discover why he kept returning. Her health deteriorated from the strain and she joined her husband in death soon after.

PALLBEARERS

Paddy Morron of Riverstown told this story to a collector for the
Schools Manuscript Collection in July 1936:

> There was a man who used to go to neighbours' houses at night
> watching other men card playing. He used to go by the fields.
> One night he was coming home when he crossed the fence out on
> to the road and immediately saw four men with no heads on them
> carrying a coffin and a girl in a white garment walking between the
> coffin and the men.
>
> The man, being very much frightened, crossed the fence again and
> the girl walked along the fence beside him. When the headless pall-
> bearers left the coffin down on the road and looked towards him he
> fainted from fright and shock. He was there for some time and when
> he revived the men and coffin had vanished. The girl remained there
> still. She told the man that these men were going to kill him and not
> to go that way again. The man knew the voice of the girl as she was a
> cousin of his own. She had died some years before that.

A GHOSTLY WARNING

Numerous incidents – too many to relate here – have been told of ghostly visitations and 'fetches', a supernatural double or apparition of a deceased or a living person. Patrick Kennedy's 1866 folklore collection *Legends of the Irish Celts* includes a brief account of *The Doctor's Fetch*, in which a fetch's appearance signals death for the titular doctor.

There are many variations on the theme such as that of a Liggin, County Sligo, woman whose only son emigrated to America, as was not unusual at the time. He died shortly afterward and the woman was inconsolable with grief. Unable to sleep, she often 'used to get up out of her bed at night and look out the window. In the dawn light she saw him on many occasions walking across a path through the fields that he often walked prior to his leaving'.

T. McG of North Sligo married a girl shortly after jilting an old girlfriend. She was heartbroken and died on the night of the wedding. Afterwards, whenever he would go to the window at night to part the curtains, he was shocked to see her looking in at him.

When word was brought to Petie Waters of Castlegal that his brother Patrick Joseph was dead, he was not surprised: 'Oh I know that,' he said, 'he was here at four o'clock this morning. He rapped on the door and told me he was on his way. "Best of luck to you," I said.'

The visitor who brought him the news related afterwards his astonishment that somehow Petie knew of his brother's death before he was told by any earthly person.

General Michael Collins was shot dead in an ambush in August 1922 during Ireland's Civil War. According to a report in the *Irish Examiner*, when word was brought to a comrade in arms he replied: 'You need not bother; I know what you have come to tell me. Mick is dead; he has just been to see me himself.'

A HAUNTED CHURCH

John N of Townalarua had a new bicycle. It was the 1940s, so not everyone had such a good bicycle and he was quite proud of it. It had the latest model dynamo that provided good light for the road ahead. Carefree, he whistled a happy tune as he sped, homeward bound from a great night's dancing at the Elsinore ballroom in Strandhill, County Sligo.

Suddenly, and for no apparent reason, the light on his bike went out! In the darkness ahead, he was quite surprised to see that Hollybrook church was all lit up. 'It was like daylight, it was that bright,' he recalled later. There was something spectral and eerie about the scene up ahead though, something that made his heart beat faster. As he came closer, he could see a horse-drawn carriage outside the gates and a crowd of people milling around as if at a funeral. He was alone and the sight frightened the wits out of him; it was three o'clock on a pitch-black night. Who were those people and why was the church lit up at this hour? Could this be the death coach – the *'cóiste bodhar* – he had heard the old people speak about?

Peddling furiously past the nightmarish scene, he recalled later that his clothes were soaked with sweat when he reached Ballinafad. Once past the church, the light on his bike functioned normally again. In later years he passed the church many a time, but never again witnessed anything like what he had seen on that night. Nor could he ever come up with any rational explanation for the lights, the coach, or the people gathered there in the wee small hours of the morning.

A Midnight Mass

In the townland of Lecklasser on the Sligo-Leitrim border stood an old church where Drummons National School now stands. Lights were often seen there at the dead of night. Mary McGovern often went there to pray after her day's work was over and one night, while she knelt in front of the altar, wearied from her labours, sleep overcame her. There was a pale moon that night that limed the green meadows and purple mountains of the bleak countryside, draining them of colour. Dimly illuminating the interior, the moon's glow beaming through the small window formed a pool of light on the floor of the church.

Startled awake in the small hours by a bright light that suddenly flamed on the altar, she looked around. To her amazement, the sacristy

door opened and a priest in full vestments silently emerged and climbed the steps to the altar. Turning around with outstretched arms, he gazed down the chapel as if expecting something or someone. Waiting a short while he turned, descended the steps again and returned to the sacristy. The lights went out, darkness descended on the church and Mary was left wondering if what she had witnessed was real or if it was a dream.

Curious now, she returned the following night to see if it would happen again. This time, wide awake, she hid at the back and, sure enough, shortly after midnight the lights came on, the priest ascended the altar as before, waited, and then retraced his steps to the sacristy. The following day, and not sure if she was going to be ridiculed, Mary described to the local priest what she had witnessed. The priest listened attentively and, when she was finished, advised her to go back another night. When the ghostly priest turned around again on the altar, she should ask him in the name of God if she could do something for him.

Mary returned and waited until the scene was repeated as before. She was frightened, but thinking of the priest's advice, plucked up courage. She was ready.

'Can I help you, father?'

The sound of her own voice echoing through the silent church startled her still further. The priest looked straight at her.

'Thank God,' he replied. 'For years I have been trying to say a Mass for someone who gave me an offering.'

He explained he couldn't offer the Holy Sacrifice without a server. Neither could his soul go to rest until he fulfilled his earthly obligation. Although Mary had never served Mass before, she attended the priest anyway and was surprised when it came as easily to her as if she had being doing it all her life. When the Mass was over, the apparition disappeared from view and even though Mary often went back to the church after that, she never again saw anything out of the ordinary. She was ill for some time after the experience but when she recovered, people said she could ever afterwards 'serve Mass with any of the best trained young boys in the parish'.

THE WHITE WOMAN OF LIOS

Cards was more than a game at McGowan's in Lecklasser – it was a passion. Gambling went on all night until morning's rays quenched the oil lamp's gleam. Weary from a night spent playing and smoking around the kitchen table, James Gallagher stretched himself and parted the blinds. It was just breaking day and he was astounded to discern the figure of a woman looking in at the house. She raised her hand in a gesture meaning that he should say nothing.

Fear compelled him to hold his silence that morning but he couldn't keep the secret for long. Eventually he revealed what he had seen to his companions. They were not surprised. They had heard that a figure called the 'white woman of Lios' was often seen on the old road. It frequently entered a byre in Lios townland at night while a woman there was milking her cows. On one such visit the spirit asked for milk and, receiving it, promised the woman that it would never harm her or anyone belonging to her. They believed this was the person or spirit Gallagher had seen. That finished the card playing at McGowan's. The owners made wooden shutters and installed them on the windows to block out the sight of the spectre.

Shortly afterwards two men, McGee of Carnduff, County Sligo and McCormack of Tawley, were returning home in their pony and cart from Manorhamilton, County Leitrim. Passing by Lecklasser, they knew nothing of the white woman of Lios so they were unconcerned when they saw a person dressed in white at the side of the road. 'Come away for a jaunt,' McCormack shouted jokingly at her. Immediately she started to follow them. She never spoke, so after a while the two men became uneasy as they sensed that this was no ordinary creature. There was something eerie about her.

When they came to Brocky Bridge she disappeared, and the two men heaved a sigh of relief to be rid of her. Spirits cannot cross water, so they reckoned she was thwarted in her pursuit by the stream that ran there. They were soon disappointed, however, for when they re-crossed the stream at O'Beirne's bridge, she reappeared.

She continued to follow the two men until they reached home. Unharnessing the pony in feverish haste they tied it in the stable, went into the house as fast as they could and bolted the doors. When a great knocking was heard on the doors and windows, they knelt down and prayed. They heard the pony break its tying in the outhouse so one of the men, plucking up his courage, took the tongs in his hand and went out into the yard. He called on the ghost to come forward in the name of God. He commanded her that if she had any nearer friends than him, to go to them or to some other place where she would stay forever.[6] The commotion ceased immediately.

That was not the end of it, for when McCormack looked for his pony in the morning, he found it drowned in a nearby stream. It was conjectured that the spirit had entered the body of the pony. When the animal died, so too was the spirit destroyed. Whatever transpired on that night we can only guess, but we know for sure that the white woman of Lios was never seen in Lecklasser again.

A SEVERED ARM

Driving from Sligo to Dromohair along Lough Gill, numerous motorists had the eerie experience of a hand and arm with no body attached placing itself on the dashboard or reaching for the steering wheel. One witness thought that it was a joke; someone had hidden in the car

and was playing a prank. But there was no one there. On arriving in Dromohaire, he told his amazing story but no one was surprised, telling him it was a frequent occurrence.

Another driver remembered that on the night it happened to him, he was driving a Wolsely motor. A disembodied hand crept up on the dash as he was driving past a spot near Parke's Castle. When he put his hand over it, there was nothing there and no one in the car. The manifestation was accompanied by 'an indescribably terrible smell'. He had heard that Sir Frederick Hamilton of Manorhamilton was said to have murdered a person at this spot many years before and dumped the body in the lake. Since that time strange things have happened and, 'people have got an eerie feeling at this place'.

BRACKEN'S GHOST

Local workers employed at the gamekeeper's lodge on the Classiebawn estate in Mullaghmore feared to be left there alone. It was haunted, they said, by the ghost of a caretaker who lived there years ago. When he died, the old people said, they couldn't get his hands into the coffin.

Chancing to look out the window, they saw him there with his hands held up over his shoulders. He was often seen afterwards, a shadowy figure walking past the window, keeping a lonely vigil. Sometimes a heavy step was heard inside the house, making its way across the upstairs floor and down the stairs, 'every step like a ton weight'. A cautious search of the house revealed nothing.

A door leading to the kitchen could never be closed. Thomas B----rambled there in the evenings with the gamekeepers Watty and Jules Bracken.[7] On a stormy night he asked them 'Why don't ye close that door? There's an awful draught going through the house.'

'You can close it if ye like', Watty responded, smiling, 'but it won't stay closed.'

'What are ye talking about?' Thomas replied, laughing. 'Of course it will. What'd be wrong with it?'

He got up, closed the door and sat around the fire resuming the conversation with his friends. After a while, the door swung open. Thomas looked at the other men incredulously. Examining the latch and finding it in good working order, he shut it again. Again it opened wide of its own accord. Thomas left the door alone after that and offered no explanation to me other than to wonder if the door might have been in the path of the old caretaker doing his nightly rounds.

SODEN'S GHOST

Old fishermen seemed to have an endless supply of stories that happened in times past. One of these was often told by Jamesy Charlie Gallagher about the ghost of the landlord and priest-hunter Soden from Moneygold. He recalled how a demon spectre had wrought great mischief when the Mullaghmore boats were out fishing herring at night. He and his fireside listeners marvelled at the priest who, following appeals from the frustrated fishermen, banished the devilish presence to Bomore Island's bleak and barren rock.

Soden had gone raving mad following a confrontation with the local curate, a Fr Rynne, following which 'he ate his own flesh and nothing could be done with him'. Jamesy explained:

The priest was saying Mass above along the river there at Grange, near where the Tech is now. Soden was the landlord in Grange; he was living where Kilfeather's shop is now. Someone informed on the priest, as there was a price of £5 on their head then, that there was a crowd of them saying mass up at the Mass Rock. Soden sent the yeomen out right away, arrested the priest and brought him down. I heard me father at that hundreds of times, that oul' history. When he tried to sign the warrant to execute the priest he wasn't fit, he went clane mad, the priest was never executed.

Following Soden's descent into insanity he was locked in a disused Revenue Police barracks in Grange, County Sligo. Later known as Lang's Shed, it had barred windows and doors but was demolished around 2004 to make way for a new housing estate. The Loughlin family from nearby Caiseal, charged with his care, fed him his meals through the bars. Because of his violent nature, his food was delivered at the end of a pitch-fork. Once a week they tied him to a lone blackthorn tree in a nearby field, 'in order to scrape the lice off him'. The tree still stands.

Soden lived for about a year after the incident. Following his death, reports went out of a 'huge black dog with fire coming out of his mouth' seen at Hood's Gate near Soden's property. At night, people went around by the fields rather than pass the spot. In the daytime, passers-by hung rosary beads on the handlebar of their bicycles for protection. Horses pulling sidecars or traps reared up and stood trembling when they came to the haunted spot. It happened to the O'Connors of Moneygold, but thankfully Mrs O'Connor had the presence of mind to say a prayer: 'Go on, in the name of God', she said to the horse, upon which the horse calmed down and went ahead.

Locals called on Fr Rynne to do something about the spectre, upon which he exorcised the unquiet spirit to the open sea a few miles away. The phantom dog disappeared following Fr Rynne's intervention – but that wasn't the end of it. The following winter fishermen from Mullaghmore went to the priest with a strange story. Something – they believed it was Soden again – was interfering with their nets and tan-gling them as they fished herring at night. Could he do something to help them?

The priest went to the seashore and, performing the exorcism again, banished the tormented and tormenting demon to the bleak and barren Bomore Rock, 10 miles out to sea. Legend has it that his ghost still resides there but is allowed to return to the mainland once every seven years.

There are those who will testify that they have witnessed the home-coming. On a calm summer's day, with no living thing to be seen, or enough wind to stir a leaf, they have heard noises like 'a herd of ele-phants or horses' crashing through the woods on the old Soden estate. They believe it was caused by the phantom landlord making his way to his old haunts from where he was originally banished.

'A ghost is compelled to obey the commands of the living', W.B. Yeats once wrote. 'The stable boy up at Mrs. G----'s there met the master going round the yards after he had been two days dead,' an old country-man told him. The lad said, 'be away to the lighthouse, and haunt that; and there he is far out to sea still, sir. Mrs. G---- was quite wild about it and dismissed the boy.'

For those who felt they had been wronged, the placing of a curse on their oppressor was the only resort left to the persecuted of those harsh times. There are many examples of harm coming to tyrants by mysteri-ous means; in this instance, the priest was the avenging agent.

According to a recent report in the *Irish Times*, exorcisms are still performed today and, furthermore, the Catholic Church is introducing new rites for expelling demons. An exorcism is a ceremony of prayers in which a priest, with the approval of a bishop, casts out an evil spirit, calling on it aloud to leave a person or place. Speaking from Rome, Cardinal Jorge Arturo Estavez confirmed the modernisation, affirming that, 'demons are fallen angels as a result of their sin, and they are spiritual beings with great intelligence and power.'

Father Malachai Brendan Martin, author and priest, stated that, 'Exorcisms can be extremely violent. I have seen objects hurled around rooms by the powers of evil. I have smelt the breath of Satan and heard the demon's voices – cold, scratchy, dead voices carrying messages of hatred'.

COURTHOUSE GHOST

It is true that some stories can be explained away by natural means: coincidence, roguish invention or such. Do not, however, make the mistake of supposing they are all old wives' tales, mischievous concoctions, or a product of fevered imaginations. Tomorrow's experience may make a believer of the most hardened sceptic. The spirit world runs in a parallel dimension to our own and requires very little to cross over. Neither can we take comfort from the thought that these ghostly happenings are a thing of the past; that they couldn't occur in our 'enlightened' age. Historical knowledge sometimes gives substance to something imagined. Quite often the reverse is the case and substance is given to unbelievable stories by subsequent archaeological investigations or discoveries.

Padraig Feeney lived with his wife Una near the village of Rathlee. On passing a certain section of the Cabra road a sense of distress and foreboding repeatedly welled up within Una. The feeling was so strong and persistent that eventually Padraig and Una, in order to avoid this area altogether, were forced to take the long way around when travelling to Easkey or Ballina. With no logical explanation for the feeling, Padraig's curiosity was aroused and he decided to investigate. On making enquiries in the neighbourhood he soon discovered that a gruesome murder had occurred at a house in this locality many years before. Only a few scattered stones remain now to mark the spot.

The spirit of a locality, we believe, can radiate from inanimate things. A place that was lived in, or suffered in, is forever stamped by that living; by the joys, the anguish, the human struggle. It bears an imprint like a person's soul, an *anima mundi* of the earth that can never be extinguished. Its being is intact, forever pulsing within it have we but the faculty, the instinct, to draw from it as water from a well. Una, it seems had tapped into that primeval link.

When workers at the old courthouse in Sligo town told of hearing a buzz of noise and voices in the courtroom at dead of night people were sceptical. Surprised that the court would sit at such a strange hour, the workers investigated and, on entering the room, were puzzled to find it empty and in complete darkness.

Disturbed by the experience, they recollected afterwards an oppressive atmosphere and 'a cold, clammy feeling' in the air. On numerous occasions an ethereal, headless figure was seen travelling, not at night as is usual, but often in broad daylight, from a point near the stairway along the corridor to a window where a 'hanging judge' once looked out on executions ordered by him in the courtyard below.

Images conjured by overwork or lack of sleep were blamed by scoffers, who had not witnessed the apparition – until excavations carried out by Mr Eoin Halpin of Archaeological Services uncovered skeletons beneath the floor. The discovery was reported in *The Irish Times* of 20 May 2000. One set of disarticulated bones was found at the very spot where the ghost habitually commenced his restless wandering. The skeleton, like the uneasy phantom, was headless! Was this, then, the unsettled spirit of some tormented creature whose screams of innocence were choked off forever when his neck snapped at the end of the hanging judge's rope? No evidence as to the identities of the remains has yet come to light.

THE FRIENDLY GHOST

Irish ghosts seem for the most part to mind their own business. Rarely have they been shown to be hostile. Yet the very thought of someone coming back from the dead, friend or foe, instills in us an anxious dread. There is no reason for fear – and yet, unbidden, it rises within us. 'It's the livin' ghost ye have to be afraid of!' people would say loudly, as if trying to convince themselves, and they'd know there was truth in it, but deep down in their trembling hearts the fear clung.

Ghosts, like people, have their favourites and their idiosyncrasies. They take to some people better than others. The record for the friendliest ghosts must surely go to a place called Grange on the borders of Sligo and Roscommon. Killavil man Pat James Duffy got the story from his aunt, who lived there.

Her neighbour, Michael John, had lived in England for years. He didn't much like it there, so when he had saved enough money he returned home, about 1955, and bought a two-storey house in Grange that belonged to the 'landed gentry' at one time. Michael didn't know that it had a reputation of being haunted. No one else would buy it; several other families had come to live there and had to leave because of interference. Furniture was thrown all over the place, footsteps were heard on the stairs, beds were lifted in the air. It had lain empty for years, an auctioneer's nightmare, until Michael came along, an auctioneer's dream. Michael was delighted with his bargain. Pat's aunt was appalled when she heard the news: 'Michael John,' she said, 'What in the name of God did you buy that house for?'

'What's wrong?' he replied, 'Isn't it a great bargain at eighty quid?'

'Didn't the people who lived there before you have to leave because of all the noises and disturbances in the place?'

'I'm not worried about that,' he said. 'They'll do me no harm.'

'Do you hear anything at night?'

'Of course I do,' he replied, 'but so long as they're not bothering me, I'll not bother them.'

Some years later, when electricity came, he bragged to Pat's aunt that the ghost switched the light on for him every time he returned home. She thought this was a very funny joke until one night he told her to come and see for herself. Sure enough, when they came within about ½ a mile of the house, the lights came on.

'They must like me,' he said, 'They have nothing against me, anyway.'

9

MERMAIDS

A mermaid found a swimming lad,
Picked him for her own,
Pressed her body to his body,
Laughed; and plunging down
Forgot in cruel happiness
That even lovers drown.

- W.B. Yeats

Merrow (from the Gaelic *murúach*) is the Scottish and Irish equivalent
of the mermaid and mermen of other cultures. They seem to have been
around for millennia, as according to the bardic chroniclers, when the
Milesians first landed on Irish shores, the *Maighdean Mhara* or sea
nymphs played around them on their passage.

Perhaps the best-known Sligo tale regarding mermaids comes from
the village of Enniscrone. A mile or two south of the village in the far
west of Sligo, there is a group of round boulders hidden in the brush
beside the road. These are known as the Mermaid Rocks. Many centuries ago, Thady Rua O'Dowd was elected chieftain of his clan after his
father died. His first task, before he could take up the new position, was
to find a bride. This he soon found to be a difficult mission. Given his
position, there were many to choose from, but he found that those he
liked most were cold towards him and did not wish to marry.

One morning while out walking on the beach, as he rounded the bend at Scurmore, he saw a most beautiful maiden. She was sitting on a rock, combing her hair and singing a haunting sea song. The O'Dowd knew at once that she was a mermaid, and that the cape she sat on was the element that allowed her to switch between human and mermaid. It was a classic case of love at first sight. He knew that mermaids, if they could be persuaded, made the most faithful and loving wives. It was common knowledge that if one can only get possession of this special article of a mermaid's costume, she at once loses her aquatic nature and becomes an ordinary mortal.

Thady crept up close to the beautiful creature from the sea and, taking her cloak, made his feelings known to her. He told her of his dilemma, and promised he'd love and take care of her if she would marry him. She returned his love and they were soon married. Thady was the happiest man in the world that day and for many days and years to come. Despite this, he hid the fishtail cloak to ensure his wife would not be tempted to go back to the sea because, while she seemed happy with him, he feared he would lose her if she discovered it.

Their first spring came, daffodils grew, nature blossomed all around his fort at Castleconnor, and Eve – for that was her name – bore him the first of seven fine, strong and healthy children. Season followed happy season in their idyllic setting and their family grew big and strong. When the youngest was able to run and leap like a hare, Thady felt secure enough to leave his fort for a period. Before he left, he checked the spot where the cloak was hidden, and placed it in an even more secure hiding place. The youngest child spotted Thady at this task and was struck by the manner in which – as he gazed on it – the article flashed, glistened, and changed hues. In his innocence, he told Eve where his father had 'hidden a bag of gold before he went away'.

Curiosity overcoming her, Eve looked and, to her astonishment, found her fishtail cloak. The longing to return to the sea rose strongly in her breast, and even though she fought the impulse, she felt compelled to go. Gathering her seven children, for she could not bear to leave them, she set off for the sea at Scurmore where she had first met Thady. Resting on top of the hill above Enniscrone, Eve and her children viewed the beautiful golden strand below. Considering her position, she realised that she could not take all seven children with her. They tried to stop her returning to the sea, but its call was so strong that Eve could not resist. Being now re-endowed with all the attributes of a mermaid, she touched each of her children in succession, changing five of them into rocks. These granite boulders can be seen to this day, close to the road at Scurmore, and are known as 'The Children of the Mermaid'. Eve and the two remaining children moved silently towards the seashore, and on the way, one of those was also turned into a rock. When she reached the water, she placed the youngest snugly inside her cloak and swam joyfully out to sea to meet the friends of her youth.

She was never seen again and it is said that the boulders weep each time an O'Dowd passes away.

***

My father, Petie McGowan, often told of the night his boot got caught between two boulders while in search of *eadáils* (flotsam) along the seashore. An incoming tide crept, advancing very slowly, inch by inexorable inch, threatening to drown him. Heartbeat by heartbeat, the torturous minutes – or could it be hours – went excruciatingly by; his foot swelled, each wave inched higher and still higher and he prepared to die. Stretching, choking and inhaling seawater, he went under, again and yet again, and still the boulders held him fast. The sounds of wind and wave faded away; losing consciousness, his body relaxed and a great peace enveloped him.

He would swear afterwards that just before his eyes closed for the last time, he saw what looked like a mermaid – for her appearance fitted descriptions he had heard – sitting on a rock combing her hair as she watched him. He held out his hand to her as the mists closed in and the roar of the sea faded away. His eyes closed and he moved swiftly and smoothly from the horror.

Suddenly, it was a bright summer day. He emerged to a placid, sunlit landscape, where the sun glittered on a tranquil sea. He was free, floating, as light as air, a part of the scene, and yet not. He was in a surreal, parallel world. He saw everything clearly, as if from a height, but yet heard no sound. There was a strong scent of roses. He saw a prone body, his own, lying by the shore. The mermaid sat by the body, watching, smiling. Touching him, the strange creature hovered for a moment, moved to the water's edge, slid into the sea and disappeared beneath the waves. The light darkened, the dream faded and suddenly he was lying above the high water mark, barefoot, soaking wet, exhaling seawater from his lungs and gasping for breath. Pulling himself up on hands and knees, he looked around: the sea still raged among the boulders, the wind blew fiercely as ever but there was no mermaid, nothing to show that anything at all unusual had just happened.

The next day, he went back at low tide and found one of his boots wedged in the stones; he never found the other one.

***

Here along these barren places, among the mist and sea fog, strange things happen. Country people feared to bathe in such quiet places on a Sunday. Mermaids came up on the rocks on that day and might take them away. If you looked out on the sea, you might be mesmerised, drawn into it and away.

'Them things can happen,' Johnny Cummins once told me.

Sometimes, if you saw a mermaid, it was a sign someone was going to drown. My brother Francie was going along the shore under Classiebawn one day an' didn't he see one, like a woman with a fishes tail, that's the truth. She was up on the rock, Francie stood looking at her – he didn't know what to do – an' she went into the water again. I often heard it said when they're seen it's a warning of some kind.

The next day, the grandest day that ever was seen, and no ground swell, there was a drowning over on the back Strand behind Cliffoney. Fr Rattigan that was going on for a priest that time, he was with them. They couldn't be saved. That finished the bathing there. There's fierce holes over on that strand. They were pulled out and a wave came then and pushed them further out again. I often think about it.

The little fishing village of Raughley lies nestled on the shore in Sligo Bay on the approaches to Sligo Harbour. Just a few miles away from

Lissadell House, the birthplace of the Countess Markievicz, it was the pilot pickup point for shipping entering Sligo.

Many years ago, a man fishing near the harbour saw in the failing evening light what he perceived to be a fine fish just under the surface of the water. It had been a poor day's fishing and he thought to himself that his luck was in at last. Quick as a flash, he drew back and struck it a mighty blow with his harpoon. But the fish was strong and tried to get away. After a short struggle, his grip on the harpoon failed and he lost both harpoon and fish.

Some weeks later, he was working at hay in a field close to the shore when a well-dressed gentleman on a horse approached him and requested that he go with him. The man did not recognise the stranger and declined. The stranger was insistent, though, and after some time the fisherman was persuaded. He would go with him on one condition: that he be left back at his workplace in the field. This was agreed and they both set out on the horse. Breaking into a gallop, horse and rider sped across the fields, down to the shore and, plunging into the sea, swam some yards before descending into an underwater cavern. The man was terrified but felt powerless to resist. It was as if he was under a spell.

When they entered the cavern, there on a bed lay a beautiful woman. The sheets were bloodstained and soon the man, his eyes adjusting to the light, noticed her face contorted in pain and his harpoon stuck in her side. They both pleaded with him to pull out the object, explaining that it was only he who had struck the blow that could remove the object from her flesh; otherwise the mermaid, for that is what she was,

would die. The fisherman did as he was bidden and on removing the harpoon, was returned to the field again.

Before leaving, the rider told the man that, on account of his cruel deed, he would not have allowed him to live had he not been forced to give a solemn commitment to returning him to his place of work. He turned his horse and, riding back to the shore, disappeared beneath the waves.

ROSSES POINT

Although the teller of these stories is unknown, they were told in 1929 and took place in Rosses Point:[8]

> I'll tell you what happened to myself and John McGowan, Michael Carty and Mickey Haran a couple of years ago. We were fishing outside Carrickfodha (long rock) shortly after Mr Flood got his mowing machine, and at twelve o'clock in the night didn't the mowing machine begin to work along the 'skelp'. The three of us heard the machine going and turning, and we could hear the cracking of the driver's whip and the snortin' of the horses as plain as if the machine was working within a few yards of us. Now, you may not believe it, but it's as true as there's a God in heaven. And I'll tell you another experience, just as surprising. We happened to be out fishing on Martin's Night or as it's called, Old Hallow Eve, and we forgot the night it was, as we never fish on either Hallow Eve or Martin's Night. Suddenly we saw another set of nets close beside ours. There are corks on the back ropes, which keep the nets upright, and in the 'swing' and as soon as we look the nets which we saw so plain beside ours at once disappeared. We then let go again and at once the strange nets appeared, again, and began to 'foul' with ours. At last we hauled in our nets altogether … and we were only about a mile from the shore, but before we could reach land a storm suddenly overtook us, and we were all nearly lost.[9]
>
> Every man that was in the boat can tell you all about it, as well as me. And you bet none of us ventured out on a St Martin's Night again. An'

the same men can tell you as when suddenly a whole building, which is three times as high as Flood's three-storey house, appeared in a blaze, with fire and smoke coming out of every window, and the light from it was so bright that you could read a newspaper in the boat, although it was a pitch-dark night. We got frightened and hauled up the boat on the shore, and we walked all the way up to Ballisodare. Next morning when we returned, the ould building was there just the same as ever. And maybe you wouldn't believe that every seventh Hallow Eve night, every window in Walker's lodge is in a blaze of light, although no person has lived in it for many a long year.

I ought to tell you as well about the mermaid that myself and John McGowan and Mickey Haran saw on Bowmore strand. We were fishing on that particular night outside Bowmore, when suddenly we saw a white figure standing in the water between the net and the shore. As we were hauling in on the strand, the object glided over the top rope of the net, and passed close to Mickey Haran. It was swimming or sailing against both wind and tide, and John McGowan, who was at the lower end of the boat, and who has a lot of the daredevil in him, left the rope to me and crossed up towards the bow to catch the figure. Haran stopped him, lifted his oar and swore he'd brain him if he went a step further – that it was enough for them to mind their own business, their fishing, and let mermaids alone. Both of them are still living witnesses and can tell you the same as I'm telling you.

Although I don't believe much myself, said John McGowan, in fairies or ghosts, I must give in that it's true, every word about the mowing machine working away on the rocks at midnight; and that the mermaid appeared to the three of us outside Bowmore Strand, and that I would have caught her only for Mickey Haran. Yes, there are some queer things to be heard and seen sometimes about this place.

10

St Patrick
in Sligo

Miracle at Coney Island

The Coney Island seaside resort and beach in Brooklyn, New York City, is very well known. The original Coney Island, which lies in Sligo Bay and gave its name to the New York version, is not so well known. So what is the connection and how did it come about that the two islands so far apart have the same name?

New York's Coney Island came into popular use in the first half of the nineteenth century, after a ferry service was instituted to carry passengers across Coney Island Creek at that time a waterway separating the island from mainland Brooklyn.

An Irish sea captain, Peter O'Connor, sailed the schooner *Arethusa* between New York and Ireland in the late 1700s and named Coney Island after an island of that name near his home in Sligo. This Coney Island was, and is, about 1 mile long and about ½ a mile wide – much like the American version.

The island, being a natural habitat for rabbits, takes its name from them: *Inis Coinín* (Island of the Rabbits), anglicised to Coney Island. There is an old saying: *Is feárr greim de choinín ná dhá greim de chat* (one bite of a rabbit is better than two of a cat).

For a small island, Coney is rich beyond its size in heritage and lore. Abounding in stories of fairies, mermaids, saints and sages, there you will find St Patrick's Wishing Chair, St Patrick's Well, the remains of a washed-up whale and forts where the fairies live. As we have seen, long before St Brendan (and later Columbus) discovered America, St Patrick was brought to Ireland as a slave. Escaping his captivity, he returned many years later as a Christian minister. He travelled the length and breadth of the country, telling people about Christ and Christianity and baptising the Irish race so that most of them became members of the church of Christ. Everywhere he went, old customs and pagan rituals were deeply embedded. Instead of outlawing the old ways, St Patrick wisely blessed them and gave them a new Christian meaning.

The old Gaelic customs for honouring and welcoming guests were held in high esteem, and travellers were welcomed and given food and shelter. St Patrick's welcome on Coney, however, was qualified and whatever goodwill there was went downhill rapidly after the deceit of an island woman was exposed. It took a minor miracle to bring the trickery to light.

For years following this miracle at Coney, the incident became known as the Day of the Rabbits. Cana in the Holy Land might have its changing of water into wine, and Bethsaida its miracle of the loaves and fishes, but what was that compared to the miracle at Coney? Mind you, when one realises that rabbits didn't officially come to Ireland until the Normans brought them in the twelfth century, the miracle at Coney was doubly astonishing. When this incident happened, the Normans were still running around herding goats and rabbits, living in mud huts and minding their own business somewhere in Europe. They had not yet beaten their ploughshares into swords.

Like so many things in Ireland, the story begins with St Patrick. Following a disappointing visit to Calry where he not only failed to Christianise the people who lived there, but to add insult to injury had his pet deer eaten by the natives, Patrick headed off in high dudgeon for fresh and hopefully more productive fields. The story was handed down for centuries. Joe Neilan (1893-1976) of Sligo town remembered hearing it from his father:

'Ye killed the deer that followed us from Tara, an' I was fond of that deer,' the holy man declared when he found all that was left of his pet. 'Well,' says he, 'I'll leave Calry but remember this, ye'll always be poor people here. From Monday morning till Saturday night it'll be from hand to mouth with ye.' With that, he left Calry in disgust.

'I'm going to Coney Island now,' says he, 'and I'm going to build a church there on the very point of it, and I'm going to call that church Killaspugbrone. It'll be the first church consecrated in the west of Ireland and I'm going to put Bishop Brón in charge of it. He's a native of this district here, a native of Coolera under Knocknarea.'

Patrick travelled on and when he came to Coney Island, he was hungry and tired. He came to the house of a family called Mulcladhaigh, or 'Stone' in English. Presenting two rabbits to the woman who greeted him, he asked her if she would be good enough to cook them for his dinner.

The woman had heard about Patrick and she didn't like a lot of what she heard. Who could blame her for being suspicious of this foreigner with his new ideas about an even more foreign god. Didn't she already have a religion? Wasn't Crom her god?

'Ye're supposed to be a saint,' she says, 'we're not saints here, we're pagans, and when you leave we'll still be pagans. We don't believe in your Gospel.'

Patrick was hungry and not in the humour for a religious debate. First things first. He could preach the gospel later, when he had a full belly.

'Will ye cook the rabbits for me anyway,' he says, 'we're hungry.'

'I'll cook the rabbits alright for you,' says the woman.

She took the two rabbits out to the back of the house, gutted them and washed them. They were fine fat rabbits. While she was skinning them, she came to thinking that she'd like to have them for her own dinner. They'd make a better meal for decent people than this rambling preacher. What she had was cats, lots of cats.

So she hit on an idea.

She caught two of the cats, killed them and cleaned them. When she was finished you couldn't tell which was a cat and which was a rabbit!

Joe picks up the story:

She went over an' put all into a big pot on the fire. She put a red twine, homespun wool, around each of the necks of the rabbits and dropped the two rabbits into the pot along with the cats. While the

rabbits was boiling she put a few vegetables into the pot along with
the rabbits an' the two bloody oul' cats. After a while she poked the
rabbits to see if they were done:

"Now they're boilt," she says, "ye can have your dinner."

'Course it was in Irish she was talking; there was no English in
them days. She lifted the two cats out of the pot an' she went over to
a big dresser in the kitchen. She took down two big wooden plates an'
she put one whole cat on a plate for St Patrick along with vegetables
an' whatever else.

St Patrick looked at her, he had a suspicion of her, an' he looked
at the 'rabbit' that was on the big plate. What did he do but put the
sign of the cross over the rabbit an' as soon as he did, the bloody oul'
cat jumped off the plate and out the door. There was two dogs in the
house an' away with them after the cat. He went over to the pot and
put the sign of the cross on it and out jumped that cat too and out
through the door. Away with them and the two dogs and the two cats
disappeared an' never was seen after.

St Patrick looked at her again and he says:

'Woman Stone,' he says, 'ye have a heart of stone an' this island is
called after you: *Inishmulcladhaigh*, Stony Island, *Inishmulcladhaigh*,
the Island of the Mulcladhaighs. Well, forever ye'll be pagan. Unless

when I have the church in Killaspugbrone finished that I'll be able to get ye baptised.'

The very day the church was finished, the minute Patrick went into it, his tooth fell out an' they called that tooth *Fiachal Padhraig*, St Patrick's tooth. That tooth was enshrined an' it was the greatest shrine that ever was in Ireland. It's above in Trinity College in Dublin.

The woman was awed when she saw what Patrick had done with the cat and how her trickery of substituting cat stew for rabbit was exposed. Full of remorse for the trick she had played on Patrick, she came to him the next day. 'I think I'll be baptised a Christian,' she said, 'but the rest of my family won't. We argued and argued all night to no avail, but I see your point, I'll become a Christian.'

When she was baptised, Patrick looked at the rest of the family and pronounced a curse: 'You're here for generations on this island,' he said, 'and the island is called after you, *Inishmulcladhaigh*, but there'll never be one of your name a clergyman. Nor will there ever again be four of your name in this townland to carry a corpse. There'll come a time when there won't be one of your name on *Inishmulcladhaigh* again, an' that'll be very soon.'

Patrick's curse came to pass. Tradition has it that before he left Sligo, the Mulcladhaighs of Coney Island had all died out.

St Patrick's Arrival in Sligo

The arrival of St Patrick in AD 432 swept away the old religion practiced by Queen Maeve, her subjects and her followers. Patrick spent seven years in Sligo out of a total of twenty-seven years spent on his mission of conversion in Ireland.

Passing his youthful years as a slave to the Ulster chieftain, Miliuc, it was from Sligo that Patricius, as he was then known, made his escape aboard a ship bound for Gaul. Arriving home to Roman Britain, he studied for the priesthood and, following his ordination, obeyed the message revealed to him in a dream that he should return to Ireland.

The Irish already had a religion, and Crom Cruach was their God. They were not going to be pushovers for this itinerant proselytiser with grand notions of establishing a foreign god.

Patrick first set foot in Sligo at Geevagh, in what is now the Barony of Tirerill. Four holy wells in the locality dedicated to his name bear testimony to his mission. The ruins of an ancient church near Ballinafad are all that now remain of the very first church established by the saint in Sligo. The stone structure replaced an earlier wooden building, as was common.

Having established a church at Kilmanagh near Lough Gara, he crossed into Mayo. Here, having climbed Croagh Patrick, he spent forty days and forty nights in prayer and fasting, at the end of which, it is said, he banished Ireland's snakes into Lough na Carra.

They haven't been seen since!

The tradition of climbing the mountain on the last Sunday in July, known as Garland Sunday or Reek Sunday, is still alive and well. In a magical, modern mixture of Christian piety and pagan superstition, thousands make the ascent through the night and early morning, many in their bare feet. The custom was ancient even in St Patrick's time, when people travelled there on the Festival of Lughnasa to honour the Celtic god, Lugh.

The leaders of the old religion, alarmed at Patrick's success, were determined to have a showdown. It is said that when Recradus, the chief Druid of Mayo, heard that Patrick was headed in his direction, he made preparations. Following a meeting with the other druids, he decided to ambush the saint and kill him. Killing people you didn't like was big in Ireland then. When Patrick saw Recradus approach with 'nine Druids clad in white garments and with a Druid host', he wasn't a bit concerned. Raising his left hand to God, he cursed the druid, who immediately dropped dead in the midst of his magicians. As if that wasn't enough: 'As a sign of punishment he was consumed by fire in the sight of everyone.'

Making his way to Sligo over the River Moy, Patrick and his train of servants were stoned by a hostile mob at Bartragh Island, who presumably hadn't heard about Recradus. Turning to the stone-throwing mob, he cursed them and, we may say, rather unfairly cursed their descendants as well, for good measure.

Word had gone ahead, so when he got to the Sligo side of the river the druids were waiting for him, and they were in a bad temper. Three of their best men were assigned to put an end to Patrick, but their efforts had no effect. Casting aside their spells and poisonous concoctions, he proceeded north and made camp at Carrowmably near Dromore West.

During his stay in Sligo, Patrick established Aughris, Dromard and Killaspugbrone. Countless sacred wells of the old religions were Christianised. Tobar Tullaghan, 3 miles west of Ballisodare, popularised by W.B. Yeats in his play *At the Hawk's Well*, is probably the best known of these. Although on the side of a mountain, its water level is said to rise and fall with the tide in Ballisodare Bay. Sacred trout swim there, but can only be seen by believers. Although they have been caught, cooked and eaten by the philistines, they are miraculously restored to the well where they swim serenely about as if nothing had happened.

Patrick was a great man for dispensing blessings, as you might expect from a saint, but as we have seen, he was a dab hand at the cursing too. In his search for converts, he distributed both with abandon. Maybe it's what the Irish understood best: the whip and the olive branch.

Fishermen came in for a lot of abuse from Patrick. A supply of food was a constant worry for the saint and his followers, so when he encountered fishermen at river crossings, he saw this as an opportunity to stock up. However, the hardworking men often didn't see why they should part with any of their hard-earned catch to what looked like, what we might call in modern times, a bunch of hippies.

On his way north through Sligo, he passed over the River Duff on the Sligo-Leitrim border. Seeing men fishing there for salmon, he asked them if he could have some.

'They're scarce today,' was the reply from the tight-fisted Leitrim men.

Big mistake!

'May they always be so,' replied the disgruntled holy man. That finished the fishing there for a long time.

Leitrim has a very short shoreline, so presently St Patrick and his followers came to the River Drowes, which separates County Donegal from County Leitrim. The Cassidy family and their helpers were fishing for salmon. Still hungry, Patrick begged them for a fish, which they immediately gave him. Perhaps they had heard about the incident up the road. Patrick had his dinner and he was grateful. Blessing the river, he said: 'May the Drowes never be without a salmon nor a Cassidy to catch them.'

'And,' says the *Tripartite Life of St Patrick*, 'even little boys take fish there still, and a salmon of the Drowes is the finest of Ireland's salmon.' The Drowes continues to be a popular fishing spot as it generally produces the first salmon of the year. The Cassidys owned and fished the river up to very recent times.

Christianisation continued in the sixth century and St Colmcille founded the churches of Emlaghfad in the barony of Corran and Drumcolumb in Tireril. The remains of a round tower and high cross at Drumcliffe in the barony of Carbury reveal that this too was an early Christian site of major significance, founded by St Colmcille in AD 575. In the adjacent churchyard, the mortal remains of W.B. Yeats lie at peace in the Sligo soil that inspired much of his work.

How St Patrick Banished the Last Serpent out of Ireland

March is the month when we celebrate the bringing of Christianity to Ireland by St Patrick. For most people nowadays, it has little religious significance at all and indeed in many places, including Ireland, it has become a pagan *bacchanal*. Let's go back to more innocent times, then, and find out how St Patrick outwitted one last obdurate, wily old serpent.

St Patrick, by the power of God, had driven all the snakes out of Ireland. Those that could not be driven out were allowed to stay, but they had to submit to being turned into conger eels, with all the venom washed out of them. There was one big wise old snake of which St Patrick could not get the better, however. He could neither lead, drive nor coax him, and, mind you, he was in quite a pucker about it. Following many sleepless nights, Patrick hit on a plan. He got a big box,

and with great ceremony placed it in front of his altar on top of Croagh
Patrick Mountain. The old snake was not far away and, half in and half
out of his hole, kept an eye on the saint out of the corner of his eye. You
see, he didn't want to give Patrick the satisfaction of knowing that he
was worried and so pretended not to notice what was going on. Still,
after a while, curiosity got the better of him and he asked, 'What are
you going to do with that box, Pat?' By this time, the two were on first-
name terms, or at least the old serpent thought they were. The two had
been adversaries for a long time and the snake, while he would never
admit it, had a sneaking regard for St Patrick and his abilities.

'That's my business', answered the saint, abruptly.

'Civility costs nothing,' replied the snake sharply, quite offended by
Patrick's rebuff. 'It's not much of a box anyway, when all's said and
done.'

'It's big enough to hold you, you old bag of bones,' said Patrick taunting his slithery opponent.

'That's a lie for you,' said the snake taking the bait, 'the half of me
wouldn't fit into it.'

The saint didn't bat an eye: 'That's as it may be,' he answered, as mild
as milk, 'but I'll bet you a bottle of *poitín* it would hold you with no
trouble at all.'

'Done with you,' said the serpent, 'but you're not to try any tricks
with the crook of your staff if I come out of here.'

'Honour bright,' said the saint and put the staff away behind a rock.
The serpent came out of his hole and began slithering into the box,
swelling himself to twice his natural size until the box was full. A good
bit of the end of his tail was still sticking out and he was quite pleased
with himself to have won the bet. 'There now for you Pat, I knew
I would win, now what do you think of that?'

With that, St Patrick slammed down the heavy lid of the box all of a
sudden. The snake didn't have time to get out of the way or out of the
box, so he whipped his tail in, afraid it would be snapped off. In two
seconds flat, the saint had the key turned in the lock, lifted the box to
his shoulder and with a mighty heave, flung it out into the Atlantic.

And that is how the last serpent in Ireland was outwitted by St Patrick.

St Patrick, the Hawks Well and Caorthannach, the Fire Spitter

The Hawk's Well at Tullaghan, on the slopes of the Ox Mountains, is one of the wonders of Ireland. Its origin is attributed to St Patrick. As we have seen above, it is well known that, from the peak of what is now known as Croagh Patrick in County Mayo, Patrick banished all the serpents and snakes out of Ireland and into the sea, where they drowned (excluding, of course, those that were turned into conger eels as we have already noticed).

In addition to those already mentioned, there was another demon serpent that managed to escape. This demon was known as *Caorthannach* (sometimes called the Fire Spitter) and claimed to have been the Devil's mother.

The demon slid down the side of the mountain, thinking that she was unobserved. But St Patrick saw her, and was determined that no such fiend should remain in Ireland. This demon would not be as easily fooled as the others, however, so at the foot of Croagh Patrick, the fastest horse in County Mayo was brought for Patrick to ride. Mounting this steed, he set out at once in pursuit of *Caorthannach*, the Fire Spitter.

The demon sped northwards, spitting fire as she went. She knew that St Patrick would need water to quench his thirst as he travelled, so she poisoned every well that she passed. The saint became more and more thirsty as he pursued the demon but, knowing that he must not drink from the contaminated wells, he rode on until he reached Tullaghan in County Sligo. By now, he was so desperately thirsty that he prayed for a drink.

Suddenly, his horse stumbled on a rock and St Patrick was thrown to the ground. As he fell, his hand and back struck a stone and where he landed, a well sprang up beside him. The water from this well was fresh and safe to drink and the saint drank from it until his thirst was quenched. Then he hid himself in a hollow beside *Carraig-an-Seabhach* (Hawk's Rock) and waited for the Fire Spitter to arrive.

As the demon approached, St Patrick sprang out and banished her with one word. The Fire Spitter drowned in the Atlantic Ocean and the swell she created flowed into the well. Ever since then it became a healing well and ebbs and flows with the tide, containing alternately fresh and salt water, as if connected to the ocean.

This legendary property caused Giraldus Cambrensis in 1188 to name it one of the wonders of Ireland: 'A well there is of sweet water; the property of that well is, that it fills and ebbs like the sea, though it is far from the sea.' The mark of St Patrick's hand and back, where he fell from his horse, and the imprint of the horse's hoof, can still be seen on the stones by the well.

The *Book of Ballymote* (1391) relates: '*Seal do lo 'ina saile searb glas, Seal aile 'na huisgi glan, Co fuil 'na hingnad 'san Eri, Tibra indglan Slebe Gam*.' ('One part of the day it is salty, bitter and grey, another while it is fresh water so that it is a wonder in Ireland, the tarnished well of the Ox Mountains'.)

The site, also known as Tullaghan Hill Holy Well, was once an important place of pilgrimage, where the devout trekked up the steep slope to the well. It looks out over the same scene that W.B. Yeats conjured in his stylised drama *At the Hawk's Well* (1916), the first English play to use the dramatic form of Japanese Noh Theatre. In this one-act play, the dried-up Tullaghan Well is reputed to periodically hold water that would make whoever might have a taste immortal. The hero Cú Chulainn arrives, wishing to have a chance at living forever. But an old man, who had been waiting there for fifty years for the well to fill up, tells the hero about his wasted lifetime: whenever the well filled with water, an enchantment caused him to fall asleep and miss his chance to drink and gain immortality.

Many legends are associated with the Tullaghan Hill Holy Well, one of which is that water taken from the well cannot be brought to a boil. Another legend concerns a pair of enchanted trout, not visible to everyone, which appear primarily for the faithful. These fish never grow old and are held to be very sacred. If they are removed by unbelievers, they are said soon afterwards to be seen again swimming peacefully in the well, as noted by Lady Wilde in 1902:

> ... A tradition exists that a sacred trout has lived there from time immemorial, placed in the well by the saint who first sanctified the water. Now there was an adventurous man who desired much to get possession of this trout, and he watched it till at last he caught it asleep. Then he carried it off and put it on the gridiron.

The trout bore the grilling of one side very patiently; but when the man tried to turn it on the fire, the trout suddenly jumped up and made off as hard as it could back to the well, where it still lives, and can be seen at times by those who have done proper penance and

paid their dues to the priest, with one side all streaked and marked brown by the bars of the gridiron, which can never be effaced.

Originally, harvest celebrations were held here to celebrate the pagan goddess Áine; they have continued to recent times as a Christian festival. Here then we have this most remarkable well, a well that has been regarded as sacred for more than 2,000 years, that saw the seamless changeover from worship of the gods of the pagan world to those of the new Christian religion

11

A NOBLE
HORSE

A horse interred in consecrated ground? In a Catholic cemetery? Surely
not, I hear you say! But go visit Ballyara graveyard in Tubbercurry today
and there you will find proof of this remarkable occurrence.

The Mullarkey family held lands – around 800 acres – in the barony
of Leyny, County Sligo in the 1870s. At the time of Griffith's Valuation,
Patrick Mullarkey was leasing over 130 acres from the Ffolliott estate at
Ballyara, and almost 300 acres from the Phibbs estate, both in the parish
of Achonry. In 1870, Michael and Margaret Mullarkey offered for sale
lands in the parishes of Achonry and Ballisodare in the Landed Estates
Court, and over 280 acres of lands at Drumartin, barony of Leyny,
in the Land Judges' Court in June 1885. The sale notice indicates that
the property at Drumartin was originally held on lease between Eliza
Cooper and Patrick Mullarkey, dated March 1790. The family are also
associated with a famous racehorse, called Pride of Ballyara. He won
them substantial monies in the mid-nineteenth century and is buried
on the perimeter of the graveyard in Ballyara. Here the family owned
land which is now the site of St Attractas Community School. Some
claim the horse is buried *in* the family plot but the evidence for this is
inconclusive.

Pride of Ballyara was retired to Ballyara in 1845, after his racing career
was over. Shortage of food was severe in Ireland over those years as the
potato blight killed the staple crop of most of the native farmers and
incredibly much food was exported out of the country. The Mullarkey

family purchased large quantities of oats, maize and corn in England
and had several shiploads transported to Ballina port for distribution to
the needy throughout South Sligo. Horse and cart was the only means
of transport then, and a severe shortage of horses meant that Pride of
Ballyara had to go into action, pulling cartloads of grain over a 50-mile
return journey. The respect the Mullarkey family – and the people
of Tubbercurry – had for this great horse caused him to be buried in
Ballyara Graveyard. A large memorial stone erected in his honour, reads:

> The Pride of Ballyara
> Tread softly oe'r this spot
> If blood can give nobility
> A noble steed was he
> His sire was blood
> and blood his dam
> and all his pedigree
>
> This slab is in remembrance
> of a famous thoroughbred
> that netted a fortune
> for the Mullarkey Family.
>
> In Black 47 the famine yrs. Dr. J.P. Mullarkey purchased 2 cargoe
> of oatmeal and 2 cargoe of potatoes and carted to Drumartin Aclare,
> Tubbercurry as a gift. We shall ne'er meet his like again.

The Famine Years of 1845–1847 were severe in South Sligo, as in other
parts of the country, and but for the help of a local merchant family –
the Mullarkeys of Teeling Street – things could have been a lot worse.

12

COMMUNICATING
WITH RATS

Can rats be persuaded by reasonable discussion to quit an area? Although regarded as pests, some have great respect for their intelligence. Believing they could understand human speech, many farmers would not speak out loud of what they planned when putting down traps in case the rats might hear. It was held by some that if you wanted to rid an area of the rodents, all that was needed was to stand near the entrance to their holes and tell them where they could find other accommodation. But they were fussy; it had to be an improvement on where they were.

A wise man might make sure that the new home was across running water as rats, like witches, detested it and would be unlikely to return, even if they didn't like the new place. In County Tyrone and in Antrim, it was judged prudent to find the head rat and address any such advice to him.

The practice of talking to rats was not confined to Ireland. In France, a special formula was used: 'Male rats and female rats, I conjure you by the great God to go out of my house, out of my habitations and to betake yourself to England there to end your days.' In 1943, in the US, *Colliers* magazine published an account of similar practices by farmers in Maine.

In *The Golden Bough*, Sir James Frazer quotes an ancient Greek tract on farming, which advises anyone wishing to rid their lands of mice to take a piece of paper and write on it: 'I adjure you, ye mice here present, that ye neither injure me or suffer another mouse to do so. I give you yonder field [specify the field] but if ever I catch you here again, by the

Mother of Gods I will rend you in seven pieces.' Enough to intimidate a strong man, never mind a humble mouse! The procedure was to stick the paper on an unhewn stone in the field before sunrise, with the written side up.

The last such recorded banishment in Ireland happened in the parish of Riverstown, County Sligo at the end of the nineteenth century. A woman who lived near Kilross graveyard, concerned with an infestation of rats there, went to a local priest for help. She was afraid they might colonise the thatched roof of her house and so place her in great danger. The priest wrote something out in Latin on a piece of white paper for the concerned woman, with the instruction to say certain prayers for a given number of days. She was then to attach the paper to the gate leading into the graveyard.

Following all instructions carefully, she waited and watched. Some time later, to her astonishment, she saw the leader of the rat colony take the paper in his mouth. Gathering behind him, the rest of the rodents, 'swarmed through the bars of the old gate, crossed the road and plunged through into the townland of Knockatubber and were never seen afterwards'.[10]

In an incident recorded in an American magazine in the 1920s, a farmer there took a much more diplomatic approach. Appealing to the rodents' sense of fair play, he wrote a civil letter to them and pinned it up in the barn. The note advised them that the farmer's crops were short, 'that he could not afford to keep them through the winter, that he had been very kind to them, and that for their own good he thought they had better leave him and go to his neighbours who had much more grain than he'.

Tom Healy, a fiddle player from Ballymote, County Sligo, was reputed to have powers akin to those of the Pied Piper. A pleasant man who travelled far to play for dances and parties, he had a darker side for people who aroused his anger; he could billet rats with those who offended him. Anyone doubting his abilities were directed by John Kearns of Drumfin to two houses in the townland, where a plague of rats visited the occupants on the fiddler's command. Following this demonstration of his mastery, only the very brave crossed Tom Healy.

Legend has it that rats formed a part of the arsenal of Ghoibhneann, magical smith of the *Tuatha De Danaan*. The story goes that a giant who lived on the Beare Peninsula in County Cork once demanded that Ghoibhneann make a perfect razor for him. This he did, using the blood of rats to temper the steel. So effective was the blood and so sharp the razor that with one stroke it shaved off both beard and epidermis from the giant without causing any pain.

In ancient Ireland, it was commonly held that rats could be killed through rhyming verses. This power, held by the poet classes, was recognised outside Ireland and recorded by the playwright Ben Jonson, who wrote: 'Rhyme them to death as they do Irish rats.' Even Shakespeare was aware of this humane and uniquely Irish method of pest control. In *As You Like It*, Rosalind notes the charming practice of lulling rats to death through poetry. 'I was never so be-rhymed since Pythagora's time that I was an Irish rat,' she says.

The Sligo poet W.B. Yeats was familiar with this power too, and mentions it in his poem, 'Parnell's Funeral':

> ... All that was sung,
> All that was said in Ireland is a lie
> Bred out of the contagion of the throng,
> Saving the rhyme rats hear before they die ...

The ancient Irish poets exercised their power to kill lower animals through a spell called an *aer*. Senchan Torpeist, seventh-century chief poet of Ireland, holds the distinction of being the first person on record to apply this unique power. Once, when his dinner was eaten by rats, he uttered an *aer* on them which began: 'Rats though sharp their snouts, are not powerful in battle ...' It is recorded that, following this contemptuous slur, ten of the hairy mischief-makers dropped dead on the spot. Noble rats, no doubt, who were so humiliated at such an insult to their valour that they just fell over and died!

An age of honour, warriors and heroes indeed – even in the rat world.[11]

13

POWER OF
THE PRIEST

Strange powers were attributed to priests. Up until the 1950s, they were regarded with awe and fear, and with very good reason: they ruled with an iron hand. Whether they were right or wrong, it was a brave man, or a foolhardy one, who crossed a man of the cloth. It may seem strange now but many were convinced that clerics had the power to put horns on them, or worse, if they incurred his displeasure. It was commonly held that, 'If ye'd raise yer hand to a priest, ye'd lose the power of yer hand.' Men could be pointed out whose hands had withered away after raising them to threaten or strike a priest.

Father Devine of the parish of Ahamlish was one of these strict disciplinarians, whose very name instilled fear. When death called, as it did at every house sooner or later, irrespective of disputes or disagreements, the priest was summoned to ease the soul's passage to the next world. Father Devine's strange power manifested itself on one such sick call.

Max B---- was a young boy when he was sent to the presbytery to bring the priest to his uncle, who was dying. It was a dark, windy night.

'How am I going to get up to the hill road without a light?' the priest demanded.

'I dunno', Max replied.

'Did you bring a lantern?'

'No.'

Fr Devine went inside, lit a candle, and handed it to Max, instructing him to lead the way.

To his astonishment, and despite the wind, the candle remained lit on the journey to the sickhouse. The priest anointed the dying man and the pair returned along dark roads, their way again lit by the candle. When they got to the presbytery, the priest handed the light to Max, telling him to take it with him. When the door shut behind the priest, the candle went out and the young boy made his way home in the dark.

Rumours have persisted over the years that this place, once home to the 'landed gentry', is haunted. Visitors there have sensed a woman rushing by them in the hallway, heard a whish of robes, seen nothing but felt a clammy coldness. Fr Doyle was among several priests who admitted to being aware of a 'Presence' there. Was this then another incidence of the restless spirits mentioned in Seamus Deane's book *Reading in the Dark*, 'a relic of our war torn history'?

***

There was this family in Bunninaden and they had a pick on the parish priest. They were of a different religion and used to be out jeering and mocking him when he was saying his prayers. Fr James Henry was his name.

Shortly afterwards they were out winnowing oats and commenced to bring in the oat stacks – but try as they might they wouldn't budge. Reluctantly they came to the conclusion that the priest had something to do with it.

Even more reluctantly still they decided that there was nothing for it but to go to the priest and ask him if he had anything to do with it. Denying that he was in any way responsible he nevertheless, in response to their pleadings, consented to go to the field with them. When he got to the field he went up to one of the stacks and left his cane on it.

After that they had no bother and went on with their harvesting, but I'm telling you that put an end to the mocking![12]

***

Achonry is reputed to be one of the most historic areas of Christianity, dating back to the fifth century. This area boasts traces of the first monasteries built on a small stream on land known locally as 'Scanlons'. During the Penal Times a monk travelling on foot from this monastery to another, namely Churchill in the parish of Bunninadden, was surrounded by Cromwellian soldiers. On his refusal to hand over the Blessed Sacrament, he was attacked & killed at a place in Tubberdur, known as *Mullach an Chrois*. There is a cross carved on top of his grave where, remarkably, the grass never grows and the cross clearly visible to this day. An open-air Mass is celebrated there annually in August on the Feast of St Nathy.

***

There was a priest in our town one time used to keep geese. Didn't a local fellow, oh he was a bit of a vagabond, steal one of the geese. The family gave out to him so much that he went to confession:

'Father,' he says, 'I stole a goose, I'll give her to you.'

'You'll do no such thing,' replied the priest, 'I'll not take her.'

'But, but …' hesitated the penitent.

'Never mind now,' replied he priest sternly, 'you'll have to give her back to the person you stole her from.'

'Well, I offered her to the person I stole her from and he wouldn't take her.

'Is that so? Well, you can keep her yourself so,' said the priest.

***

Many years ago a man named Paddy Cullen lived near Cliffoney village. One sunny autumn day, he was quietly digging potatoes in his field when the parish priest came walking along the road. Curious about his parishioner's work, he asked Paddy what kind of potatoes he had.

'Raw ones,' Paddy replied.

Paddy had had a disagreement with the priest some time previously and was feeling particularly sour on this day. Naturally enough, the priest wasn't pleased at all with this short answer and responded tartly, 'I wonder, do you know your catechism as well?'

'Try me,' says Paddy back to him.

The priest, rising to the challenge, enquired, 'What is baptism?'

Quick as a flash, Paddy replied: 'It was two shillings and sixpence in me father's time, but it's five shillings since you came to the parish.'

The priest smiled at the irascible Paddy and continued his walk along the road.

14

THE SHIP-SINKING
WITCH

Fishing was poor along the Sligo coast when news reached there of great catches of herring across the bay in Bruckless, County Donegal. This was the nineteenth century and there was no dole then, or State subsidy; you got nothing for nothing. Fishermen had small plots of land, where they grew their own food, but they still needed cash to pay the landlord and to buy the few essentials that could not be grown: tea, sugar, tobacco, flour.

It was usual for seafaring men to take great risks: it went with the occupation. It wasn't that there was any such thing as choice in employment. There were no jobs. You took a penny where you got it. Craft were frail, equipment patched and barely serviceable. Bruckless was a long way from home, but the men made their boats and nets ready, said goodbye to their families, and set sail.

When the Mullaghmore men got to Donegal, the herring fishing was as good as they had hoped. The weather was fine and they worked all through the night, landing their catch in the mornings. Each day, an old woman came and asked the men for herring. They knew her as Biddy. She had very little money, but gave whatever few pence she could. When she had no money left, however, the Donegal fishermen refused to give her any more fish.

But it was not because they were miserly. Fishermen worked close to nature and the primal elements. They held the sea in reverence and fear. Care was taken not to offend spirits that, although unseen, were ever watchful. Taboos were rigidly observed: to stick a knife in the boat's 'taft' or mast invited bad luck; meeting a red-haired woman on the way to a fishing trip was an evil omen; bread went unbuttered for fear of bringing misfortune; whistling was forbidden as it 'whistled up the wind': 'there'd be "a bad smell off ye" if ye whistled in a boat. Ye could play music or sing, but there'd be no whistling'.

To give goods away without receiving anything in return, they believed, was to 'give away your luck'. There was no question of taking a chance with such things. Luck, good or bad, meant success or failure, poverty or survival; the belief ran deep in the orthodoxy of rural communities. In their life's cycle many forces, mysterious and unpredictable, sinister and benign, were at work. Customs, pagan or Christian, endorsed by generations of experience, were sacrosanct. They protected against evil and the unknown. No, they couldn't just give the fish away; they had to get something in exchange.

Any small amount would do, but the poor woman had nothing. Nothing at all. Evening after evening she came to the boats and each time she was turned away. Eventually she was given fish by the crew of a Streedagh, County Sligo boat, who took pity on her. Taking the gift, she went off up the road, threatening those that refused her that they would have cause to remember their meanness. There would be a story to be told soon, she threatened.

The Streedagh fishermen lodged in the same house as the Donegal men. When they went out to shoot their nets the next evening, a Donegal boatman unintentionally donned a sweater belonging to a man named Bruen from Streedagh, County Sligo: a happy mistake that would later save his life.

The next day, Friday 12 February 1813, started just like any other day. A rosy dawn broke bright and clear over the Bluestack Mountains and Barnes Gap as the fishing fleet finished their night's work. Preparing for her revenge, the old woman watched from a cabin window on a hill overlooking the bay. She filled a milk pan with water and, placing a wooden bowl to float on it, she asked her daughter to keep watch from the window and tell her what she observed. Staring at the pan with a fierce concentration, the old woman splashed the water about in the vessel, causing the bowl to dance about.

'What do you see?' she asked the girl.

'Oh, a breeze has sprung up, mother,' she replied.

The old woman continued to agitate the water. 'What do you see now?' she asked.

'The breeze has turned into a gale,' the daughter replied. 'The men are reefing the sails. The boats are in big trouble.'

The witch, for that is what villagers later claimed she was, continued to cast her spell while questioning her daughter: 'What do you see now? Are they still afloat?'

'Yes, mother, but some have sunk and others are trying to make it to land.'

She continued to dash the water about in the pan until the girl told her mother that she could no longer see the boats. Crying out in delight, Biddy ceased her stirring. The storm abated but the fleet was completely wrecked. Some were swamped at sea, while others were driven ashore and broken to matchwood on the rocks. The old woman's words had come true. Most of the Donegal boats were lost and their crews drowned – except for the man who was wearing the Streedagh man's jumper. He came safe from the old woman's curse and lived to tell the story.

It's a remarkable tale, but is it true? Newspapers of the day do indeed carry accounts of the tragedy. It happened at Bruckless, County Donegal on 12 February, 1813. According to these reports, no accurate estimate of casualties is known. The approximation of forty-five men drowned, leaving 'thirty widows and one hundred and two orphans,' is regarded as conservative.

What caused the sinking? Was it a natural disaster, a vindictive act precipitated by the old woman's curse, or a mere coincidence? Who can say? We do know that tales of ship-sinking witches are nothing new. Approximately 1,500 years ago, the Greek play *Alexander Romance* described a similar ship-sinking rite performed by the Egyptian pharaoh Nectanebus. Perhaps this was a secret formula handed down from the ancients; a practice, like so many others, that is now lost.

When news of the Bruckless drowning reached Mullaghmore, families feared the worst. Villagers lined the shore, anxiously scanning the sea for sight of the absent boat. They lit fires on the cliffs at night to guide the fishermen home. Hoping against hope that their men would return, they prayed for a miracle but steeled themselves for a tragedy.

We can only imagine the jubilation of the watchers when word eventually went out that the Mullagh boat was sighted beating against the wind and waves as she made her way home. Hard pressed and storm driven, the crew couldn't make it to the harbour and were forced instead to head for shelter. They beached their craft at *Trágh Ghearr*, south-west of the peninsula under where Classiebawn Castle now stands.

Watchers lining the shore counted seven men on the boat as she sped along the coast behind the hill known as *Cnoc na Taoisigh*. They were relieved to see that everyone was safe, but surprised to see a woman sitting at the helm, alongside the skipper on the 'stern taft'. This created something of a stir. Maybe one of the men had met a woman over there and there might be a wedding in the offing! When they went to help the fishermen draw their boat to safety, they found only seven men, but no woman. The fishermen shook their heads when they were asked about the stranger on board. No, there were only seven men on the boat at any time. There must be some mistake. No, there was no woman. The enquirers shook their heads in disbelief. Sure hadn't the whole village seen her clearly with their own eyes as the boat went by the headland?

Following the incident, villagers discussing the strange visitation speculated that the woman they had seen in the boat was the spirit of a dead relation, guiding the fishermen safely home from the drowning tragedy – or perhaps a woman of the *sidhe*, who took the boat and crew under her protection.

The mystery of the extra passenger has not been resolved to this day. The individuals who witnessed the incident are long dead, the details barnacled and dimmed with time. The story itself barely survived. It was passed on by the recollection of one old man of the village; passed on faintly through a fortuitous 'echo-harbouring shell' of memory.

The story has another curious twist. Some time after this extraordinary deliverance, the fishermen and their relations made a pilgrimage to a place known locally as *Dostann na Bríona* near Classiebawn Castle. There they left a 'wee crockery jar of whiskey' as an offering and a thanksgiving. Why? To the uninitiated, *Dostann na Bríona* looks like nothing more than a hilly outcrop. To whom or what, then, was the offering made? There was no church there, nor even a ruin, so we can be certain it was to no Christian god!

'People used to go to the Fairy Rock, or *Dostann na Bríona* as some call it, for lots of reasons with bottles of whiskey and *poitín*,' Thomas, an old man of the village, once told me.

It was a regular thing, long ago. The offering was left at a small round hole at the top of the rock in thanksgiving for a blessing or at set times like Hallowe'en. They used to pour the whiskey on the ground or break the bottle and let the liquid soak into the soil. Whatever the reason it was done it's an enchanted place. Anyone'll tell you that! There was this fella one time brought a bottle of *poitín* up and he was having second thoughts about pouring it out. Begod wasn't it knocked out of his hand before he could think!

Quare things happened there. There was this fella one time delivering a keg of *poitín* to Classiebawn. 'Twas a nice day and he was taking his time. When he was going up past the Fairy Rock, he sauntered over to the door to have a close look at it. He got an awful hop when he heard a voice saying to him, 'Pssshth! Give us a drop of what you have with you there.'

He jumped back and made for Classiebawn as quick as he could. Before he got to the top of the avenue, the keg fell and smashed on the ground.

As it spilled on the ground, he swore he heard a laugh and a voice saying, 'Good enough for him!'

Thomas took a long pull out of his pipe. Looking at me thoughtfully for a minute, he ventured an opinion: 'Don't ye think he'd be as well if he had to take the cork off it and give them a taste? I'm thinking if he had, he'd still have had the *poitín*!'

15

SLIGO:
THE SHELLY PLACE

The town of Sligo bears a name that is on record for almost a millennium and a half. It occurs in three early and unimpeachable sources, each over 1,000 years old. *The Annals of Ulster*, considered the most reliable collection of early Irish annals, tell of a battle it calls *Bellum Slicighe*, which was fought in the year AD 543 and in which the most notable victim was Eógan Bél, King of Connacht. The form *Slicighe* is the genitive singular of *Slicech*, meaning 'a shelly place'. This tells us that it is the name of a river, most Irish river-names being feminine.

As early as the year 670, a bishop from Tirawley (in what is now County Mayo) named Tírechán wrote an account in Latin of St Patrick's missionary journeys. When recounting the saint's supposed travels in north Connacht, it mentions 'the river of Slicicha' (*flumen Slicichae*) – the name here being a lightly latinised form of *Slicech*. This, then, was the name of a river – undoubtedly the old name of the Garvogue (just as *Gaillem*, modern Gaillimh, was the old name of what is now called the River Corrib). Sligo is one of the earliest and most reliably attested of Irish place names, occurring three times prior to AD 1000 in three impeccably trustworthy sources as Slicech, exactly equivalent to the modern form Sligeach. It is on record much earlier than the name *of every other major town and city* in Ireland. For example, it occurs a century and a half before our earliest record of one of the two names of Dublin (*Áth Cliath*) and three centuries before the capital's other name, Duiblinn.

This River Sliceach (or as it is now known, the Garavogue) is fed from Lough Gill (*Loch Gile*) and joins the sea at Sligo town. It is mentioned in ancient texts as one of the 'nine royal rivers' of Ireland. Legend has it that St Patrick blessed the river so that it would produce salmon all year round. The lake takes its name from Gile, one of the nine daughters of Mananaan Mac Lir, sea god of the *Tuatha De Danaan*. Some say that on wild and storm-tossed nights, she is still seen in the vicinity of the lake over the waters of which, 'she skims in her fleet rolling chariot.'

> For o'er those waves, from time unknown,
> The enchantress fair,
> Whose name they bear,
> Hath reigned on her crystal throne;
> There her fleet chariot wheels of old
> Over the glassy waters rolled …

Lough Gill is overlooked by Cairns Hill, a wooded prominence rising to 390ft, so called because it is capped by two cairns. According to legend, these cairns are the burial places of two Sligo chieftains of olden times, Romra and Omra. Their kingdom was once the old city of Sligo, which legend tells us now lies under Lough Gill.

How could such a thing happen?

Legend tells us that one of the chieftains, Romra, had a beautiful daughter named Gile, meaning 'brightness'. Omra asked Gile to be his wife, but she refused and rejected him. One day, when it was raining, Gile went to a well in the plain to bathe. Looking up, she saw above her head the man who was seeking her. The girl died of shame and found death in the well. After her came her foster mother (some say her nurse-maid) who wept, and the tears that fell into the well made the lough. Hence it is from Gile, Romra's daughter, the lake is named.

When Romra discovered what had happened, his anger and his fury was so great that he proceeded to do battle with Omra, killing him in the battle. There Omra died by Romra's hand, in vengeance for his daughter. When he realised his loss, a gore-burst of grief broke in his breast for sorrow because of the loss of his daughter. These events are memorialised in the two cairns that still today overlook the lake: Cairn Romra and Carn Omra.

***

Sometime in the late 1800s, a man who lived beside the lake went out on a bright moonlit night to draw a bucket of water for washing up. As he approached, the waters of the lake, 'like a bright shining mirror', began to recede before him. The man, although astonished at the sight, walked out 'into a totally unknown country', with wide streets and fine buildings. The inhabitants stared, apparently just as amazed to see the intruder as he was to see them. One of them made a grab for him and they struggled, but the man, breaking the grip of his assailant, made for home as fast as he could, bolted the door behind him and fainted on to his bed. When he recovered consciousness, he wondered if it had been just a dream. Looking down, he saw that he still held in his hand 'a curiously shaped bottle, having a pungent odour' that he remembered taking from a table of a house in the buried city. This he showed for many years to anyone that doubted his story.

Come to the lake on cold and frosty winter mornings and you will see a ghostly smoke rising from the waters of Lough Gill. An English tourist once asked a Sligo boatman, who had rowed him from the town to the lake, if he had ever seen those buildings of past ages under the waters.

'I surely have,' was his reply, 'and still on a clear day, won't you see the smoke from the chimneys rising straight up in the air from the surface of the lake.'

Legend has it that it rises from the chimneys of the lost kingdom submerged under the lake that was once ruled over by the tragic chieftains Omra and Romra.

THE WELL OF TOBERNASHELMIDA

Can such an event ever happen again? According to legend it is within the town of Sligo, in the district once known as Knocknaganny, that you will find the well of Tobernashelmida, the 'Snail's Well'. The name is derived from an enchanted or metamorphosed being, said to be seen every seventh year emerging from its waters in the form of a huge snail. This enchanted creature possesses, if provoked, the power to cause the overflowing of the well and another submergence similar to that which happened previously at Lough Gill.[13] Until recently, Tobernashelmida's waters flowed in a field near Old Pound Street on the stagecoach route that once ran to and from Sligo town. With the installation by Sligo Corporation of modern walls and footpaths, the waters of this well, regrettably, flow no more. However, we may be certain that the spring still surges underground in its Stygian caverns, beyond the will of man – as it has done since the dawn of time.

Every so often, on dark and stormy nights, passers-by have been frightened by a shapeless, swirling shadow emerging from the ground in this location. Watching in dread, they observe the apparition hover for a while before hastening in the direction of Lough Gill and disappearing from view.

16

THE LOST BELL
OF LOUGH GILL

Everywhere we go in Sligo history and legend are inextricably inter-
twined. Lough Gill is no exception.

According to another tale, the silver bell from the Dominican
Abbey in Sligo lies in its depths. Legend says that worshippers hid it
there when the friary was sacked by Sir Frederick Hamilton's men in
1642. On hearing the approach of the dreaded Hamilton, the gold
and silver vessels used in the sanctuary, along with the silver bell
blessed by Pope John XXII, were hurriedly thrown into iron-bound
chests of oak and lowered into the waters of the River Garavogue.
Those who hid it perished during the raid, so its exact whereabouts
remains unknown to this day. Sometimes, it can – particularly on the
Festival of the Holy Trinity (the first Sunday after Pentecost) – be
heard pealing out over the waters, but only persons who are free from
sin can hear the sound. It is also believed that the musical tolling of
the bells is the last, comforting sound heard by any soul drowned in
the lake or river.

Known locally as the 'Abbey', the friary was built by Maurice
Fitzgerald for the Dominicans in 1252. The sacking came about when
Hamilton, after whom the town of Manorhamilton gets its name,
and his soldiers attacked the sleeping town on the night of 1 July 1642.
A diary kept by one of his soldiers records the event:

Our colonel with his horse falling on many good houses full with
people upon this side of the bridge, he burned and destroyed all ...
it is confessed by themselves we destroyed that night near three
hundred souls by fire sword and drowning, to God's everlasting great
honour and glory for our comforts.

Moving on to Sligo Friary:

The foote met and fired their brave Mass house and Friary where it
is said we burnt many good things left by the people for safe keeping
and all their superstitious trumperies belonging to the Mass ... the

friars themselves were burnt, several of them running out were killed
in their habits; we finished this work giving God the praise for our
success ...

W.B. Yeats immortalised the event in *The Curse of the Fires and the Shadows*:

As the door fell with a crash they saw a little knot of friars, gathered
about the altar, their white habits glimmering in the steady light of
the holy candles. All the monks were kneeling except the abbot, who
stood upon the altar steps with a great brazen crucifix in his hand.
'Shoot them!' cried Sir Frederick Hamilton, but none stirred, for
all were new converts, and feared the crucifix and the holy candles.
The white lights from the altar threw the shadows of the troopers
up on to roof and wall. As the troopers moved about, the shadows
began a fantastic dance among the corbels and the memorial tablets.
For a little while all was silent, and then five troopers who were the
body-guard of Sir Frederick Hamilton lifted their muskets, and shot
down five of the friars. The noise and the smoke drove away the
mystery of the pale altar lights, and the other troopers took courage
and began to strike. In a moment the friars lay about the altar steps,
their white habits stained with blood. 'Set fire to the house!' cried
Sir Frederick Hamilton, and at his word one went out, and came in

again carrying a heap of dry straw, and piled it against the western wall, and, having done this, fell back, for the fear of the crucifix and of the holy candles was still in his heart. Seeing this, the five troopers who were Sir Frederick Hamilton's body-guard darted forward, and taking each a holy candle set the straw in a blaze. The red tongues of fire rushed up and flickered from corbel to corbel and from tablet to tablet, and crept along the floor, setting in a blaze the seats and benches. The dance of the shadows passed away, and the dance of the fires began. The troopers fell back towards the door in the southern wall, and watched those yellow dancers springing hither and thither.

For a time the altar stood safe and apart in the midst of its white light; the eyes of the troopers turned upon it. The abbot whom they had thought dead had risen to his feet and now stood before it with the crucifix lifted in both hands, high above his head. Suddenly he cried with a loud voice: 'Woe unto all who smite those who dwell within the Light of the Lord, for they shall wander among the ungovernable shadows, and follow the ungovernable fires.'

And having so cried he fell on his face dead, and the brazen crucifix rolled down the steps of the altar.

17

LUG
NA GALL

Curses are common in Irish folklore and not to be taken lightly. The antiquarian, O'Donovan, said that a curse, once pronounced, must fall in some direction. 'If it has been deserved by him on whom it is pronounced, it will fall upon him sooner or later, but if it is not deserved, then it will return upon the person who pronounced it.'

Curse or coincidence, Hamilton's murderous foray into Sligo had an interesting and tragic sequel. Just a few miles from Sligo, on the Manorhamilton road, is the enchanting Glencar Lake and valley. One of the waterfalls in this place was made famous by W.B. Yeats in his poem 'The Stolen Child'. According to the poet, the fairy folk whispered here in the ears of slumbering trout:

> … Where the wandering water gushes
> From the hills above Glen-Car,
> In pools among the rushes
> That scarce could bathe a star …

The picturesque Glencar Valley is guarded on each side by steep cliffs. Numerous streams, like silver threads on the mountainside, rush down to replenish the lake. *Sruth in Aghaidh An Aird* (stream against the height), spilling down the mountain for hundreds of feet, is the tallest waterfall there. When westerly winds blow, it is a spectacular sight as the waters defy the laws of gravity and, instead of falling down, rush in a

fountain of spray high into the air, giving it its other name: 'The Devil's
Chimney'.

On the hills high above the lake and waterfall is a ravine called *Lug
na Gall*. It was here that some of Hamilton's men, returning from the
burning of Sligo Abbey to their base in Manorhamilton, met their doom.
A party of the returning cavalry went astray in the woods, having heard
music. Following it, they found an old man sitting by a fire of sticks, his
old white horse tied to a tree. Ordering him to mount, they demanded
that he lead them on the right path for home. Putting one of the monk's
cloaks on him for a laugh, they followed their unwilling guide along a
rough path. As Yeats relates in *The Curse of the Fires and the Shadows*:

> ... the wood grew thinner and thinner, and the ground began to
> slope up toward the mountain. The moon had already set, and the
> little white flames of the stars had come out everywhere. The ground
> sloped more and more until at last they rode far above the woods
> upon the wide top of the mountain. The woods lay spread out mile
> after mile below, and away to the south shot up the red glare of the
> burning town. But before and above them were the little white
> flames. The guide drew rein suddenly, and pointing upwards with
> the hand that did not hold the torch, shrieked out, 'Look; look at the
> holy candles!' and then plunged forward at a gallop, waving the torch
> hither and thither.

The guide kept increasing his pace until eventually he signalled the
soldiers that the way was straight on from there. The ground began to
slope more and more, and their speed grew more headlong moment by
moment. They tried to pull up, but in vain, for the horses seemed to
have gone mad. Suddenly the soldiers saw the thin gleam of a river, at
an immense distance below, and knew that they were upon the brink
of the abyss that is now called *Lug na Gall* or the 'Foreigner's Leap'.
Too late! In a tangle of horses, harness and men, they tumbled over the
edge – all except for one man, who got entangled in a bush at the edge
of the precipice. Their guide, on venturing forward to see if his plan had
worked, found the entangled soldier. The latter pleaded with him to be
saved, to which the guide replied: 'If I free you, you'll kill me!'

The soldier swore not to harm the man and gave him his sword to cut him free. Grasping the sword, the guide cut loose the bush – and cried out: 'Alright, away with you with the rest of them.'

Is this just a fanciful legend? Wishful thinking? Or does this incident that happened so long ago have a ring of truth to it?

In the twentieth century, when the woods, by which the hollow is surrounded, were being planted, swords, pistols, guns, and armour were dug up. Rusted horseshoes and bits of harness also discovered there give credence to the story. As for the old man or 'guide', was he a spirit of the woods? Or perhaps an avenging angel for the White Fathers of Sligo Abbey, who were so cruelly murdered?

We shall never know.

18

THE SPLIT ROCK

Easkey takes its name from *Iascach* (abounding in fishes), a river that rises in Lough Easkey and flows through Kilmacshalgan on its way to the sea. The salmon fishery at the mouth of the river, owned at one time by the O'Dowds, was confiscated in 1617 and granted to Sir John Davys, Attorney General.

It is a curious fact that the River Easkey abounds in salmon, while none are to be found in Lough Easkey. The reason is said to be that while wading in the river, St Patrick slipped on a salmon. Immediately he cursed it, and since then no salmon has gone upriver past that point.

On the right bank of the river are the ruins of the Castle of Roslea. On the left may be found fragments of the old castle of Castletown. Built in 1207, Roslea was a stronghold of the MacDonnell, Gallowglass mercenaries of the O'Dowd of Tireragh.

On the road from Carrowmably to Easkey is the 'Split Rock'. The rock is a huge chunk of gneiss, 6 meters long by 2½ meters high, carried from the Ox Mountains by the retreating glaciers. Many people may describe it as an 'Ice Age erratic', but if the legend is anything to go by, it is much more than that.

Fionn Mac Cumhaill once arrived at the top of the Ox Mountains in Sligo with another strong man named Cicsatóin. Spotting two great boulders nearby, an argument broke out as to which of the men was the strongest. Cicsatóin challenged Fionn to throw one of them into the sea at Easkey. Normally this would not have been much of a challenge to Fionn but his wife, Gráinne, had recently run off with a young man named Diarmuid, so he had other things on his mind that day. He made the throw, but his boulder fell short and landed where it may still be seen, just across the road from Killeenduff National School. Cicsatóin hoisted his boulder into the air and with a great roar, lofted it far away into the sea, where it made a mighty splash.

As to Fionn, when he saw that he had lost the wager and was made to look a weakling, he took off down the mountain in a towering rage. Reaching the boulder, he split it in two with one mighty blow of his sword.

Over the hills the giant strode,
And he looked at the distant Atlantic broad.
He stood on the mountain, he aim'd at the sea
And a rock from his right hand flew over the lea.
… the stone fell short, and the giant's wrath
Was kindled fierce; the rebel rock
With his long and ponderous sword he struck,
And the granite mass was cleft in twain,
Which there from time unknown has lain,
With its wide yawning chasm, on Easkey's plain

- Mrs Godfrey

The curious may stop to examine the rock, but if they pass through the split twice, be warned! It will close and crush anyone foolish enough to go through a third time.

19

WILLIE REILLY AND
THE CAILÍN BÁN

The love story of Willie Reilly and Helen Ffolliot has all the ingredients of the great romantic classics: a spurned suitor, a rich, titled, arrogant father and a forbidden love between his beautiful daughter and a poor tenant farmer. A fictional version of the tale, *Willie Reilly and his dear Cooleen Bawn*, was immortalised by writer and novelist William Carleton (1794-1869).

The story itself is played out among the picturesque countryside surrounding Lough Arrow in South County Sligo and centres around Hollybrook House, owned by the Ffolliot family. The Ffolliots had vast estates in Worcester in England and were granted lands in Ireland during the Cromwellian Confiscations of the seventeenth century. As recently as the 1870s, John Ffolliott had over 4,000 acres in County Sligo as well as over 1,400 in Leitrim and 1,700 in Donegal. The last of the Ffolliots, unmarried sisters Mary and Margaret, sold off what was left of the estate in the 1920s and went to live in England.

The saga begins with Squire Ffolliot returning from a trip to Boyle in the year of 1841. Losing his way on the Curlew mountains, he was accosted by an outlaw known as the Red Raparee. Raparees were active all over Ireland in that period. Famed in verse and in song, they were Robin Hood-type characters who, having been dispossessed of their lands, took their revenge by robbing the class that had robbed them:

… Ah, way out on the moors where the wind shrieks and howls
Sure, he'll find his lone home there amongst the wild fowl
No one there to welcome, no comrade has he
Ah, God help the poor outlaw, the wild rapparee.

He robbed many rich of their gold and their crown
He outrode the soldiers who hunted him down
Alas, he has boasted, they'll never take me,
Not a swordsman will capture the wild rapparee …

A local man, Willy Reilly, discovered the robbery and tussled with the raider, allowing Ffolliot to flee the scene. Grateful to his rescuer, Ffolliot later sought him out and invited him to dinner. Here he met – and fell in love with – Helen, the squire's daughter. This being an unintended and unforeseen consequence, Squire Ffolliot was furious. To add to the dilemma, Helen was already engaged to another member of the landed class, Sir William Whitecroft.

Ffolliot set about immediately by fair means or foul to get rid of Reilly. He set out to find the Red Raparee. On finding him, he gave him a large sum of money and persuaded him to swear that the robbery was a setup to ingratiate Reilly with the Ffolliot household. On the strength of this 'evidence' Reilly was disgraced and banned from the Ffolliot manor and demesne. Helen didn't believe the evidence and continued to secretly see Reilly. Whitecroft, when he found out about the illicit affair, had Reilly arrested and his house burned to the ground.

But as of old, 'love will find a way', and the star-crossed lovers were determined to overcome all obstacles placed in their path. Reilly grew a beard and, unrecognised, managed to get employment in a lowly position on the Ffolliot estate. Shortly afterwards, Whitecroft examined the new employees and noticed that Reilly's hands did not look like the rough hands of a farm labourer. Bringing this information to Squire Ffolliot, he was overheard by Helen, who went immediately to her lover to warn him that he was on the brink of discovery. Distraught with the news, they decided they had had enough of persecution and that the only option left open to them was to elope.

A short time afterwards, having hatched a plan to escape, they procured two horses and set out together to leave Sligo behind them. Their plan failed, however, when Whitecroft and Ffolliot's men pursued and apprehended the two runaways. Helen was returned to Hollybrook, while Willie Reilly was lodged in Sligo Jail. The elopement and subsequent trial is memorialised in verse by an unknown author and the Irish *Cailín Bán* anglicised to the 'Colleen Bawn'. The '*bán*' (bawn) in the title probably refers to the colour of her hair, meaning blonde or flaxenhaired. Ffolliot is misspelled as Foillard. The 'noble Fox' mentioned in the ballad was Reilly's counsel. Following his success in defending Reilly he was, according to the nationalist politician and barrister, Charles Gavan Duffy, later appointed to the bench as a judge.

THE COLLEEN BAWN

'O rise up Willy Reilly, and come along with me
I mean to go along with you and leave this country
To leave my father's dwelling house, his houses and free land.'
And away goes Willy Reilly and his dear Colleen Bawn.

They go by hills and mountains and by yon lonesome plains
Through shady groves and valleys all dangers to refrain
But her father followed after with a well-armed band
And taken was poor Reilly and his dear Colleen Bawn.

It was home then she was taken and in her closet bound
Poor Reilly lay in Sligo jail upon the stony ground
Till at the bar of justice before the judge he'd stand
For nothing but the stealing of his dear Colleen Bawn.

'Now in the cold iron my hands and feet are bound,
I'm handcuffed like a murderer and tied unto the ground
But all the toil and slavery I'm willing for to stand
Still hoping to be succoured by my dear Colleen Bawn.'

The jailer's son to Reilly goes and thus to him did say:
'O rise up Willy Reilly, you must appear today
For great Squire Foillard's anger you never shall withstand
I'm afraid you'll suffer sorely for your dear Colleen Bawn.'

'This is the news young Reilly last night that I did hear,
The lady's oath will hang you or else will set you clear.'
'If that be so,' says Reilly, 'her pleasure I will stand
Still hoping to be succoured by my dear Colleen Bawn.'

Now Willy dressed from top to toe all in a suit of green
His hair hangs o'er his shoulders, most glorious to be seen
He's tall and straight and comely as any can be found.
He's fit for Ffolliot's daughter was she heiress to a crown.

The judge he said, 'This lady being in her tender youth,
If Reilly has deluded her she will declare the truth.'
Then like a moving beauty bright before him she did stand:
'You're welcome there my heart's delight and dear Colleen Bawn.'

'O Gentlemen,' Squire Foillard said, 'with pity look on me
This villain came amongst us to disgrace my family
And by his base contrivances this villainy was planned
If I don't get satisfaction I'll quit this Sligo land.'

The lady with a tear began and thus riposted she:
'The fault is none of Reilly's, the blame lies all on me.
I forced him for to leave his home and come along with me
I loved him out of measure which wrought our destiny.'

Out spoke the noble Fox as at the table he stood by,
'Oh gentlemen consider you on this extremity,
To hang a man for love is a murder you may see
I beg you spare the life of Reilly, let him leave this counterie.'

'My lord, he stole from her bright diamonds and her precious rings
Gold watch and silver buckles and many precious things
They cost me in bright guineas more than five hundred pounds
I'll have the life of Reilly should I lose ten thousand more.'

'My lord I gave them to him as tokens of true love
And when we are a-parting I will them all remove.
If you have got them, Reilly, will you send them home to me?'
'I will, my loving lady, with many thanks to thee.'

'There is a ring amongst them I'll allow yourself to wear
With thirty locket diamonds well set in silver fair
And as a true love's token wear it on your right hand
That you'll think of my poor broken heart when you're in a foreign land.'

Then out spoke the noble Fox: 'You must let this prisoner go
The lady's oath has cleared him, as the jury all may know
She has released her own true love, she has reprieved his name
May her honour bright gain high estate and her offspring rise to fame.'

Subsequently Willie Reilly and Helen Ffolliot (the Colleen Bawn) are
said to have married and emigrated to Australia. That may have been as
well as, given the political climate of the time, Reilly's action in rescu-
ing the landlord would not be popular with many of his neighbours.
The Ffolliots, as with so many of the Ascendancy families, are gone and
the name extinct.

The championing of true love, however, and the romantic story of
Willie Reilly and his Colleen Bawn, lives on.

20

THE ROSE OF
CAIRNS HILL

We owe much to the fireside poets, many of whose names, sadly, have not come down to us. Clay pipe in hand, they drew a rapt audience. Moulded in the tradition of the *filidh*, their skill was honed to a fine edge during the long nights between Samhain and Bealtaine.

Chiefs and kings feared the bards; they curried favour with them for fear of their sharp tongues. If someone displeased them, a quickly composed satirical verse could hold the subject up to ridicule. Their modern successors were no less respected. This was particularly true in small communities. The following excerpt from a lengthy composition criticises harsh foremen on the Gore-Booth estate in North Sligo; the sting of the overseer's lash has faded but the verse is indelible:

> ... There's another Scotchman, Pat, that has two crooked feet
> You know the lad that sets the bulbs way down at Carter's Seat.
> He wears a pair of knickers brown, vest and dark gray coat
> You could know him on the avenues for he always walks by note ...

Other yarns had no purpose other than to pass the long, dark hours until bedtime. Such was the case with this comic verse composed some time in the 1950s. Reading it, we can imagine the composer observing the romance in progress; the toing and froing, by bike or foot, of the lovestruck couple of a less than tender age and the scenario drawn from the imagination of the composer:

Oh rise up Biddy Lennon and come along with me
I mean to take you to the Ross, that's if you will agree.
I'll plant you on my bosom where the fleas parade and drill
And there a pretty flower shall grow, my Rose of Cairns Hill.

Oh Biddy, lovely Biddy, I have work for you to do
I have a creel holds twenty stone, that creel I'll heize on you.
You'll drive the cows to Garryowen and the cradle you must fill
And that's the work I have for you, my Rose of Carns Hill.

When Coronation Day is over and wee Lizzie gets her crown
It's then I'll get my pension, no less than fifty pounds.
We'll take a trip to London and we'll eat and drink our fill
And I'll introduce bold Churchill to my Rose of Carns Hill.

So rise up darling Winnie and come along with me
Put on your cloak and bonnet and to London we will flee
We'll get the ring in Hannon's forge on the way as we go down
Its glint will match the sparkle of any jewelled crown.

We will honeymoon in grandeur before returning home
To our purple heather mountains and wild Atlantic foam
We'll watch the evening sunset beyond the rippling rill
And live content together, my Rose of Carns Hill.

21

THE BLACK PIG
OF ENNISCRONE

Predating the birth of Christ by 200 years, and thought to be an ancient frontier defence and boundary of Ulster against raiding parties from the south, one of the oldest, best known and mysterious fortifications in Ireland is the Black Pig's Dyke. Running from County Down all the way through Armagh, Monaghan, and Cavan right through to County Leitrim, it has acquired a special place in Irish folklore and is, even yet, a source of marvel and speculation. Viewing it, the great nineteenth-century scholar and antiquarian, John O'Donovan, wondered at the 'terrible tusks of the huge boar that rooted the Valley of the Black Pig'.

The Black Pig Festival of Enniscrone has evolved from a similar legend that a wild boar, reputed to have magical powers, ran through the streets of Donegal, killing all in his path. It was covered with large bristles that were deadly poisonous to the touch. An evil spirit had taken possession of this old pig, which then took to attacking and eating local men, women and children. Armed with spears and battle-axes, local hunters set out to rid themselves of the vicious creature. The chase took them all the way to Sligo and on to Lenadoon in Easkey, where the beast plunged into the sea. Swimming ashore at Enniscrone Strand, it once again took to killing everyone in its path.

When the people of the area recovered from their initial shock, they came together and ran the Black Pig out of town, using long-handled spears and wooden poles. They chased it to a field in Muckduff (from

Muc Dubh, meaning Black Pig), where the wild beast was slain. It is said that one person, thinking that the poison in the bristles only worked while the pig was alive, touched the dead animal and died shortly afterwards. When the others saw this they knew there would be no feasting on this animal so it was quickly covered up with clay and stone. The mound is still there to this day.

Some years ago, in remembrance of the event, a large statue of the notorious pig was erected in Enniscrone. The sculpture, 4 metres long, 1.5 metres high and weighing 3 tonnes, was created by sculptor Cillian Rogers of Dromore West. It can be found across the road from the Diamond Coast Hotel, just outside the village of Enniscrone.

22

WATER
MONSTERS

Sea and lake monsters have, for millennia, inspired fear. One of the earliest and best-known accounts, written between AD 700 and 1000, is the Anglo-Saxon tale of the Norse hero Beowolf's struggle with the lake monster Grendel.

Beowulf was a warrior and nephew of Hygelac, king of what is now southern Sweden. He was sent to the neighbouring kingdom of Denmark, where a blood-crazed monster was terrorising the countryside, butchering and gorging itself on King Hrothgar's subjects. The bodies he couldn't eat he kept in a pouch, which he carried with him. Beowulf vanquished the brute, tearing off his arm and shoulder in the process. Victory celebrations were cut short, however, when Grendel's equally monstrous mother arrived to wreak vengeance. She killed a royal councillor and dragged his body, as well as the hewn-off limb of her son, to her underwater lair. Beowulf, a strong swimmer, pursued the creature, cut the head from the body and returned to Hrothgar's court in triumph.

John Baxter's late sixteenth-century map records the sighting by the armies of Clan O'Donnell of 'two water horses of a huge bigness' near their encampment on the shores of Glencar Lake. There are many records of human encounters with beings of the deep, some benevolent, some evil.

In the area known as the Rosses of Donegal, a water monster called the *Dobharchú* (water hound) killed and ate Sheila, the sister of Sean

O'Donnell, at a place called *Ros na mBallán*. When Sean went there to meet her, all he found was a bag of bones. Vowing to kill the beast, he laid a trap by arranging a pile of stones and placing Sheila's red cloak on top before waiting in hiding nearby. The *Dobharchú* came in from the sea at nightfall and, seeing the cloak, made for it. Sean Ruadh, as he was known, waited until the brute was almost above him, took aim and killed the animal.[14]

LOCH AN CHROI

Not all water creatures were so fearsome – but anyone encountering them needed to be wary. Approximately 13 miles on the Sligo side of Dromore West, there is a lake called *Loch an Chroi*. From ancient times, it had the reputation of being spellbound.

A farmer who had a sizeable tract of mountain and bog in that area fell into bad luck. Cattle died on him; when he replaced them, they too expired. Spring came around and he didn't have even a horse to plough the land. One evening as he walked through his property deep in thought, no doubt distraught at the turn of events that had befallen him, he noticed a black mare grazing along the lake shore.

Knowing she didn't belong to any local farmer, he decided to stable her until an owner came along. As he fed and looked after her, he became extremely fond of the mare, as she had a very gentle nature. Time went on and as no one showed up to make a claim, he worked her with plough and cart. Gradually his luck improved, his stock of cattle increased and each year the mare had a foal, for which he got a good price. He had good reason to be satisfied with his newfound fortune and traced it all to the lucky day when he found the strange horse. During all the years she was with him, he was kind to her, never having cause to strike her a blow.

One day, when riding her to the lake, preoccupied with his thoughts and impatient to get on with the day's work, he struck her with his whip. She screamed, leaped in the air and commenced to neigh loudly. Instantly, all the foals she ever reared came around her. The mare, with the man on her back and followed by all the foals, dashed headlong into the lake. The next day, the farmer's heart and entrails were seen floating on the surface of the water. From then on it was named *Loch an Chroí* (Lake of the Heart).

A similar incident happened in Lenadoon headland near Rathlee County Sligo. On his way to the well in the morning, a farmer there noticed a strange mare feeding in the field. Speaking kindly to her, he coaxed her to follow him home. Twelve years went by, no one came to claim her and each year she raised a foal, ploughed the land and was a model animal.

One evening, on returning from a day's work on the bog, he took the halter off the mare and, releasing her into the field, absentmindedly struck her with the halter. Turning around, she took one startled look at him and galloped off down the field. As she galloped, she neighed twelve times and each time she neighed, one of her foals came to her. All thirteen animals continued to gallop out of the field until they entered the sea at a spot between Killala and Sligo Bays. They were never seen again and from that day forward, the place where they disappeared into the waves is known as *Ceann Na Searrach* or Foal's Head.

THE PIG OF URLAUR LAKE

A creature resembling a 'big black boar' inhabited the depths of Urlaur Lake in the parish of Kilmovee in County Sligo. The prior in the nearby Dominican Abbey sprinkled it with holy water in the belief it was the Devil, but when the monster retaliated by spitting out a litter of *banbhs* (piglets) at them, they realised that they were no match for this creature and sent for the bishop. The bishop attempted to banish the fiend, who was now joined by a companion. To his astonishment, one of the beasts spoke. It informed the cleric that he was once his pet hound, fed on meat he refused to the poor people, 'who were weak with hunger'. The two unrepentant demons then set up a hideous screeching and kept at it until the friars went stone deaf.

The holy men were on the point of leaving the monastery for good when it was revealed to them in a dream that Donagh O'Grady, a piper from Tavraun, could help them. When, after a long search, they eventually found their saviour drunk in a shebeen, they must have thought the dream more of a nightmare than a revelation. O'Grady, equally unimpressed with the importance of his holy visitors or their dilemma, flatly refused to go anywhere until he had another few drinks.

In his own good time, O'Grady made his way to Lake Urlaur. Tuning the pipes, he took up position on the shore and commenced to play. The wild notes that floated out across the water drew the two monsters closer and closer. When they came close to the enchanted piper, a bolt of lightning from a clear sky struck them dead, thus bringing to an end their persecution of the priests, and haunting of Urlaur Lake.[15]

GRAINNE NI CONALAI AND THE *DOBHARCHÚ*

The legend of another *Dobharchú* stems from the bestial murder of Grainne Ni Conalai (often rendered as Grace Connolly) at Glenade Lake on 24 September 1722. The details were well known at one time and the ballad was sold and sung at fairs and gatherings in counties Sligo and Leitrim, as well as further afield:

> … It was on a bright September morn, the sun scarce mountain high,
> No chill or damp was in the air, all nature seemed to vie
> As if to render homage proud the cloudless sky above;
> A day for mortals to discourse in luxury and love.
>
> And whilst this gorgeous way of life in beauty did abound,
> From out the vastness of the lake stole forth the water hound,
> And seized for victim her who shared McGloughlan's bed and board;
> His loving wife, his more than life, whom almost he adored …

Some say that she went to the lake to wash clothes; the ballad claims that she went to bathe. It matters not. When she failed to return, her husband Traolach McGloughlan went to look for her. He was aghast when he found her body lying by the lake with the 'beast lying asleep on her mangled breast'.

This and the chase that ensued would have little credibility today if it were not for the tombstone marking the grave of Grace Connolly. Almost worn smooth now, it can still be seen at the old cemetery of Conwell, near Kinlough. A carving on the stone clearly shows a strange beast being stabbed by a dagger.

According to Patrick Doherty of Glenade, local lore records that the chase, which started at Frank McSharry's, faltered at Caiseal-bán stone fort Cashelgarron, County Sligo when McGloughlan was forced to stop with the blacksmith there to replace a lost horseshoe. When the enraged monster caught up with them, the horses were hurriedly drawn across the entrance to form a barrier. Giving the terrified man a sword, the blacksmith advised him, 'When the creature charges the horse, he'll put his head right out through him. As soon as he does this, you be quick and cut his head off.'

McGloughlan, and his brother who had joined him, slew the monster, following which the brothers were forced to flee on horseback from its avenging partner. Cashelgarron stone fort, near where the chase ended and the second *Dobharchú* met its gory end, still stands today, nestled on a height under the sheltering prow of bare Benbulben's head. Both monster and horse are said to lie buried nearby:

… For twenty miles the gallant steeds the riders proudly bore
With mighty strain o'er hill and dale that ne'er was seen before.
The fiend, fast closing on their tracks, his dreaded cry more shrill;
'Twas brothers try, we'll do or die on Cashelgarron Hill.

Dismounting from their panting steeds they placed them one by one
Across the path in lengthways formed within the ancient dún,
And standing by the outermost horse awaiting for their foe
Their daggers raised, their nerves they braced to strike that fatal blow.

Not long to wait, for nose on trail the scenting hound arrived
And through the horses with a plunge to force himself he tried,
And just as through the outermost horse he plunged his head and
foremost part,
McGloughlan's dagger to the hilt lay buried in his heart.

'Thank God, thank God,' the brothers cried in wildness and delight,
Our humble home by Glenade lake shall shelter us tonight.
Be any doubt to what I write, go visit old Conwell,
There see the grave where sleeps the brave whose epitaph can tell.[16]

23

BURIED
TREASURE

There was a man living at a place called Foyagues at one time and, one night, he had a curious dream. There was a well about ¼ mile from his house called Pulladypha, and he dreamt that there was treasure hidden in it. This well was guarded by a weasel with a cuckoo's head on him.

The man was to go to the well on a white horse any morning before dawn. If he succeeded in killing the weasel before it could call 'cuckoo' three times, he would have the treasure. All he had to do was put his hand in the well for it. As soon as he had the treasure in his possession, he was to jump on his horse as quickly as he could and ride away from the place, without looking back. If he did, he would lose the treasure.

He made up his mind to start out in search of it the following Thursday morning. He borrowed a white horse from a neighbour so as to do everything correctly, as he was told in the dream.

When he reached the well, he found the weasel lying beside it. He was just opening his cuckoo beak to call 'cuckoo' when the man rung his head off and killed him. He put down his hand to the bottom of the well and, after much labour, succeeded in pulling up a large metal vessel shaped something like a small three-legged pot.

He ran to his horse and, leaping on his steed's back, headed off down the road at a gallop. Before he had gone a hundred yards, though, he thought he heard something trailing behind him, as if it was tied to the horse's tail. He looked round to see what was the matter but no sooner had he done so than the metal pot leapt out of his hands, rolled down the path and back into the well.

The man went back again, thinking he would find it, but neither the pot nor the weasel he killed was to be found. The treasure, as far as we know, has remained in the well ever since.

(Told to Winnie Gunning Annagh, N.S., by her father John Gunning, Ballindoon for the Schools Manuscript Collection.)

24

NA DAOINE SIDHE
(THE FAIRY PEOPLE)

… Faeries, come take me out of this dull world,
For I would ride with you upon the wind
Run on top of the dishevelled tide
And dance upon the Mountains like a flame.

- W.B. Yeats, *The Land of Heart's Desire*

What a drab place Sligo would be without the lyrical genius of the poet laureate W.B. Yeats – and how dull the fabric of Ireland's literary, mystical and creative world without our fairy folklore.

Yeats chastised the Scots for ill-treating their ghosts and fairies. In Ireland, however, he discerned a kind of 'timid affection' between men and spirits. 'They only ill-treat each other within reason,' he said, 'Each admits the other to have feelings.'

To admit to a belief in fairies is to invite, at best, amusement, and at worst, ridicule. The search for evidence is made all the more difficult by their reclusiveness. Once, when Yeats had recourse to a medium to establish contact with them, the answer came back on a piece of paper: 'Be careful, and do not seek to know too much about us.'

Who is there that could ignore such a warning?

While we may through fear or goodwill grant them that privacy, natural curiosity urges us on to find out more about them, with or without their help. In the course of this enquiry we must call on not just the mystic poet, but also on some of the many experts who have puzzled on this over the years.

Irish folklorist and author Crofton Croker states emphatically that these ancient gods have *not* disappeared. They have only hidden themselves, he says, particularly from the casual observer. Only a flimsy veil separates their existence from our everyday life. 'A material woven with dreams and mist,' he writes, 'through which one could sometimes step, like the looking glass through which Alice enters into the other room, and men sometimes entered into the other room, the Otherworld, and they were lost, unable to find their way back, or came back still young and strong, after hundreds of years.'

'Ancient gods' then? And, yes, the evidence to support that assertion seems reasonable. Does not the Fairy Faith have the same origin as all religions and mythologies? But what proof is there to show that they are indeed, not just shadowy creatures, but in a previous existence, gods?

All civilisations have some form of belief in unseen worlds populated by mysterious beings. We can try to understand this world only by our own inadequate human experience. Christianity knows the inhabitants of its unseen world as angels, saints and souls of the dead; the Irish, while recognising the spirits of Christianity, know the people of the Celtic Otherworld as gods of the old religions, fairies and the *sidhe* or *daoine mhaith* (the good people). The Irish psyche is particularly attuned to know and feel invisible or paranormal influences. This is particularly true within the shadowy half-lights and shades, the magical environments and hidden nooks of the countryside. The inhabitants of this ancient landscape still retain a spiritual connection to the earth that is lost to the towns and cities. There, in the smoke and clatter, great multitudes of men and women are herded together in an environment created not by nature but by man.

Mention of 'noble' fairies is found from the earliest times in Irish-Celtic mythology. The Tuatha de Danaan (the children of Dana, mother goddess of Eire) are referred to in the Book of Invasions as gods who came from the west and defeated the earlier conquerors, the Firbolgs, for possession of Ireland. These Tuatha were great sorcerers, skilled in all magic, and excellent builders, poets and musicians. After many years practising the magic arts in their newfound home, they too were defeated, after a mighty struggle, by our forebears, the Milesians (the first Gaels).

At first the Milesians were going to destroy them utterly, but gradually were so fascinated and captivated by the gifts and powers of the Tuatha that they allowed them to remain and build forts and palaces within the hidden places of their choice. Here they held high festival with music and singing and the chant of the bards. Here also they mourned their exile from the lands they had made their own.

Just as we are convinced by this reasonable explanation of where the fairy folk came from, along comes a rival theory: that they were, and are, fallen angels. When you consider the antiquity of our ancient race, it seems eminently reasonable that there should be rival ideologies. After all, Irish history and mythology was an oral tradition, committed only to memory, and not transcribed until the ninth century.

The fallen angels theory, however, seems to have arrived with Christianity. The gods of the old religions become the banished of the new and the Church denounced all folk belief as superstitious. The Bible's Book of Revelation describes a 'war in heaven' between angels, led by the archangel Michael, and Satan and the forces of evil. The fairies' downfall, we are told, came about because they took no sides in this war, taking arms neither for God nor Lucifer. For this forbearance, they were not damned but shown some mercy. Their punishment was to be exiled on earth.

This explanation too has the fairies living in hills and under seas, linking this legend closely to the tales of the Tuatha de Danaan, who were similarly exiled. Perhaps, just as a country can have immigrants from many lands, the fairies too are a mixture of beings from differing backgrounds. One explanation is not necessarily exclusive of the other.

There are other, quite evident similarities in this version with the legend of the Tuatha de Danaan. While the Tuatha de Danaan filled their eternal lives with song and dance so that they could forget the loss of sunlight and their lands, the partially fallen angels did the same things to forget the joys of Heaven, which were now eternally forbidden to them.

Even so, they are often sad, it is said, for they remember that they were once angels in Heaven though now cast down to earth, and though they have power over all the mysteries of nature, yet they must die without hope of regaining Heaven. This one sorrow darkens their life, a mournful envy of humanity because, while man is created immortal, the fairy race is doomed to extinction on the Last Day.

According to Lady Wilde (Speranza), writer, folklorist and mother of Oscar Wilde, a fairy chief asked St Colmcille if there was any hope left that the *Sidhe* would, one day, regain Heaven and be restored to their ancient place among the angels. With great regret, the saint answered, 'No, you will all be damned.'

Hope there was none, he told them; their doom was fixed, and on Judgement Day they would pass through death and be no more; for so had it been decreed by the justice of God. Upon hearing this, the chief vanished with a loud cry into the hill, which suddenly became completely enveloped in bright flames. Happy they are, the fairy folk, but doomed to melt at the Last Judgement, for the soul cannot live without sorrow as well as joy.

Jimmy McGettrick of Ballymote told me once of a Catholic priest who was approached by a gang of men when out walking near the village. 'You'll not leave this spot alive,' they said, 'unless you tell us, will we get back to Heaven again?'

They must be fallen spirits, Jimmy thought. The priest wasn't sure what was the best thing to do. Thinking as quick as he could, he came up with an answer: 'If ye can find one drop of blood among ye, ye're safe,' he said.

They tried their best, and when they couldn't find any, they went away through the air, Jimmy said, 'with a loud wailing in a gush of wind'. The priest's answer, he believed, was inspired by God.

Yeats held that when priests had to make such a judgement, it was often done 'more in sadness than in anger'. The Catholic Church, he maintained, likes to keep on good terms with its neighbours, dead and alive, natural and supernatural.

How, then, do we recognise a member of the *sidhe* if we are ever so lucky as to meet one? What do they look like? It is vitally important to know – but there is no definitive answer. Essentially spirits, they can appear in many shapes and guises and although at times interacting with us, at other times may not be seen at all.

'I am bigger than I appear to you now,' a fairy told a Grange man many years ago. 'We can make the old young, the big small, the small big.'[17]

They are broadly categorised as: solitary and trooping fairies; those who like the company of others, including mortals; and the other, a solitary individual. Every so often they can be as big as mortals, but are mostly described as being small. The creature you are most likely to see is the solitary leprechaun. He is described as being a little, wrinkled old fellow with a ruddy complexion, 'usually dressed in a three-cornered cocked hat, with a leather apron over a green coat of antique cut, with large buttons. He wears trousers and white stockings, with great silver buttons on his old-fashioned shoes.'[18] Most who have seen them describe them as being about 2 or 3 feet high and having a ruddy

complexion. It is commonly believed that it is an enchantment on our eyes that makes them seem big or small.

One thing we can say with certainty is that, contrary to most of the popular images seen in books today, Irish fairies or *sidhe*, as they are also known, do *not* have wings. These depictions are the Victorian garden fairies or sprites of English folklore. Irish fairies, as we shall see, have much more subtle and sophisticated methods of transportation.

Although they live in a different supernatural sphere apart from humans, the *sidhe* or *daoine mhaith* (good people) take great notice of us, their neighbours, and for the most part coexist with we humans, who live at the margins of their world. Their dwelling place is on the earth and inside it and they have retained the ability to intervene in human affairs (mostly for good, but they can be mischievous or even spiteful at times).

If there is one thing of which the fairy world is notoriously intolerant it is interference with their sacred places: ringforts, fairy thorns, or their special hillside abodes. In every county of Ireland, there are numerous accounts of fairy retribution and Sligo is no exception.

***

Having collected stories from all over Sligo, Yeats found the people at the northern end of the county to be generally reticent. He had cousins at Rosses and Drumcliffe, but any further north and he felt himself to be a stranger 'and can find nothing'. The statement of a woman who 'lives near a white stone fort, under the seaward angle of Benbulben' was typical:

'They always mind their own affairs and I always mind mine,' she told him, meaning that it might offend them to be talking about them. 'Only friendship for yourself or knowledge of your relations will loose these cautious tongues,' he opined.

The faery and ghost kingdom is more stubborn than we know. It will perhaps be always going, and never gone. It has been my very great privilege to hear many of these stories denied to the poet and so, along-side other Sligo stories, will memorialise them here. Names in some instances are changed or obscured to conceal identities.

PLANNING PERMISSION FROM THE FAIRIES

It was common practice not so long ago to give advance notice to the fairy hosts when intending to build. Before erecting a house or byre, the corners were marked out with sticks, lime or a small cairn of stones. The sticks were burned in the fire and shoved into the ground while still hot in an attempt to keep evil spirits away. To prevent building in the wrong place, some made a wooden cross and placed it on the desired plot overnight. A common belief was that if it was shifted in the morning, you couldn't build there. Half a crown or any silver was put under the first stone laid. That was to keep the fairies away from the byre and to bring good luck.

George Martin of Riverstown had a personal experience of the necessity of building in the right place:

> Me father and grandfather was going to build this house. They were digging out the foundation when this strange man came along. That time you'd know everyone for miles around and a stranger was a rare thing. Anyway this fellow came along and without even bidding us the time of day:
> 'Ye're a bit in the way,' he says.
> 'How is that?' says they, a bit surprised at the man's insolence.
> 'Well, take my word for it and I wouldn't give ye bad advice, he says, 'ye'd want to go back a bit further.'
> He pointed out a place about fifteen feet from where they were:
> 'Dig there,' he says, 'and ye'll be alright.'
> They were a bit taken aback but thought they'd better do as they were told. They had a suspicion it might be one of the fairies was in it. On a Halloween night music had been heard round about there and fairies seen dancing. There was no fort there but it seemed to be their territory.

PATH OF THE FAIRIES

A house and land owned by a North Sligo man had a gap between the house and byre:

The old people said that this should never be blocked up. Anytime it was ever blocked up they lost cattle to sickness. He told me Bartley Gillen blocked it when he was working with cattle there and he lost several cattle while it was closed off.

Another highly respected neighbour, who might not wish to be named, told me of an experience he had in the 1950s. Wanting to enlarge his dwelling house, he tossed a wall and shed that was in the way. In the evening, while sitting down to supper, he heard the sound of galloping horses outside. Now at that time there were many horse carts on the road but you would never see riders and horses. Immediately rushing outside to see from where the sound came, he saw nothing. Many years later he was still puzzled by the incident: 'Sure what kind of horses be to be in it?' he surmised to me.

'Sure they be to be fairy horses! Whatever it was the shed must have been in their way and they got their liberation. That's all I can think of, that's the only explanation I have for it!'

PROTECTION FROM THE FAIRIES

At all times throughout the year, it was customary to give children sent on errands at night a cinder from the hearth to hold in their hand or put in their pocket to keep the fairies from them. It was especially important on November Eve to heed this, as the fairies then were at their most active. In recent times, a woman from Maugherow, County Sligo, recalled having a small bag of salt attached to the hem of her skirt or jacket as a protection against such dangers.

A pair of tongs placed across the cradle gave protection to a child, as Joe Neilan of Sligo explained:

'Oh, *agradh*', Biddy McGowan used to say, 'be the virtue of my oath *asthore*, me sister was taken away with the good people of the island [Inishmurray]. An' I'm warning every woman that has a young child on the island, never leave the house after dusk. If they go out for water down to the well or go visiting a neighbour's house; before they lave, if there's a child in the cradle, a young child, always take the tongs from the hob or the hob corner an' put the tongs across the cradle. 'Twas done with me own wife in this house. When you have the tongs across the cradle the good people has no power over that child, they can't take that young person away.

Before starting to milk, it was customary for some to squeeze the first few drops on the ground as an offering to the fairies while saying, 'in the name of the Father, Son and Holy Ghost'. Feeding the fairies while calling on the Holy Trinity may seem a contradiction, but it's a wise man who keeps all sides with him! If the cow kicked and spilled the can of milk in the course of milking, many old people would remark: 'Ah, take it for luck, maybe some poor creature wanted that!'

Enid Porter, in her book *The Folklore of East Anglia*, attributes the origins of a similar custom there to the influx of Irish immigrants during the famines of the nineteenth century. When the first lamb of the season was born, Norfolk shepherds poured some of the ewe's first milk on the ground, 'as a gift for the fairies who, if denied this, might cause later lambs to be stillborn'.

Seamus Moore of Drumfad, County Sligo, recalled the experience of a Cliffoney woman some years ago, while milking her cow on a summer's evening near Ath Sluaigh fort near his home. When she commenced her work, she could hear crying but couldn't identify the source. When she had finished milking, the cow kicked the can, spilling the contents onto the ground. It was only then, when the crying she had heard just a short while before turned to laughter, that the woman remembered she had forgotten to pay the fairies their entitlement.

THE *GLAS GHOIBHNEANN*

The dairy being such a central part of farm life, it's not surprising that there's a rich lore of stories attached to cattle and milking. One such story relates that the first cows that came to Ireland were as a consequence of the capture of a mermaid. On the May eve after her apprehension, she requested to be carried back to the strand where she was caught. Before she returned to the sea, she told the assembled gathering, who grieved to see her going, that they should gather there in the same spot on the following May Eve, when three magical cows would appear from the water. When the twelve months went by, a great crowd, having heard of the amazing prophecy, gathered by the shore. Shortly after midday, three cows emerged from the water, *Bo Finn*, the white cow, *Bo Ruadh*, the red cow and *Bo Dubh*, the black cow. When they came to the road they took different directions, the black cow heading south, the red cow northwards and the most elegant one, *Bo Finn*, making her way to the Royal residence at Tara. It is from these three cows that all the cows in Ireland are descended.[19] There are many places named after *Bo Finn*, such as the island of Inishbofin, off the coast of County Galway.

There are echoes of this legend in the story told to Francis Crean of Ballintrillick, County Sligo, by his grandmother:

Once upon a time there was a great scarcity of milk in Ballintrillick and Glenade. It was a time of great hunger and famine in Ireland. During that time a white cow used to come out of the sea at Mullaghmore and make her way to the stricken townlands. She gave an endless supply of milk until each house had received enough for its needs. This continued over a long period of time, the white cow returned again and again to supply the whole area with milk.

Eventually a selfish woman in the townland of Drinaghan, wishing to have all the milk for herself, decided to milk the cow dry. After she had taken enough milk for her own needs she proceeded to make sure that no-one else would have as much. She continued milking, and milked, and milked until the milk overflowed and ran into the local stream. Still she continued to milk until the stream turned white and after a while contained more milk than water. The greedy woman milked on until finally the cow ran dry. Immediately following this the cow returned to the sea at Pollyarry in Mullaghmore and was never seen again.

This story of the benevolent milk cow is a variation of a legend well known in England and Scotland as well as Ireland. The Irish version has its origins in the *Glas Ghoibhneann* (the grey of Ghoibneann, the smith-god), a famous cow of plenty that appeared in times of crisis to provide poor people with a supply of milk. She is often associated with holy wells, some of which are called *Tobair na Glaise*. An enchanted cow arrives mysteriously and gives milk to all who need it until someone annoys her or abuses the privilege, at which she departs and is seen no more. This otherworldly cow is said to have appeared at a holy well in County Donegal called *Tobar Bride*. She gave a quart of milk to everyone there until people quarrelled about who should own her, causing the beast to disappear.

MISCHIEF

Some were more attuned to and considerate of the Otherworld than others: 'There was this woman and when she raked the fire at night,' I was once told, 'and before she put the wet sods around the ashes, she pulled out some of the hot *griosach* (embers) and put it aside for the fairies, "there, let ye warm yerselves there now till morning," she would say.'

Ruined walls are all that now remain of another house in Bunduff, where the Daly family lived. Owen raked the fire before retiring at night, only to find that 'it was all scattered away in the morning'. Believing there was a message in the mischief and respecting the unseen forces at work, he started to put down a good fire before going to bed. This seemed to please the fairies, as ever after that, when a fire was lit at night, it still blazed away heartily in the morning. Neither was there any turf missing as might be expected; when it was raked, it was 'all thrown away'.

'They were honest people that would not make anything up,' a neighbour replied when I questioned that such a thing could happen.

A FAIRY WAR

A long time ago, there was a very old forge in the village of Cliffoney, where the Post Office is now located. An interesting legend was told about this. One night, the blacksmith was awakened by a knock at his window and, on getting up, found a strange gentleman waiting to have his horse shod. This the smith did, but being of an inquisitive turn of mind and perhaps for the sake of conversation, he asked if the stranger came far, or if he had far to go that night. The gentleman replied that his journey was a long one; he was on his way to help his friends in a big battle to be fought before dawn in the Donegal hills.

The smith thought this very strange; stranger still when the man added: 'If we win, I shall call on you as I come back; if we lose, the water in St Brigid's Well will be blood red at twelve o'clock in the day.' Then he went on.

On going to the well at the prescribed hour, the smith found the water blood red, as predicted. The stranger was believed to be one of the fairy host.

INTERFERENCE WITH FAIRY FORTS

Incidents of misfortune falling on the heads of people who interfered with fairy forts or fairy thorns are so numerous they would fill a book in themselves. But how does that make sense, you may ask? Were not these forts fortified places of residence built by mortal families who lived in Ireland in medieval times and before?

History tells so; commonsense tells us so – and yet there it is, count-less incidents of bad luck and even death following those who go against ancient belief: cattle, horses and people dying as a result; a man's hand withered away that had set potatoes in the fort; another lost an eye after being pricked by a thorn from the bush, while yet another man took shelter in a sandpit, only to have it cave in on top of him. A woman of Maugherow told me of a man who cleared away a fairy fort. 'There was seven of a family in the house, not one of them survived.' The story is typical.

Some got a warning, like the man who, seeing blood come out of the bush when he penetrated the bark, went away and left it alone. Or the men who went out one day to demolish ancient ruins in the shadow of Benwisken Mountain and went home in wonder when: 'The thunder and lightning came and it lit up the whole place on a calm day with not a cloud in the sky.'

People who were respectful came to no harm. A woman of Skreen in County Sligo told me: 'My father, God rest him, would never mow inside a fort, no matter how much he was persuaded. When he was finished mowing a field, he would leave the last bit of a swathe, or at least a few *traithníns* (wisps) for the fairies.'

INTERFERENCE WITH FAIRY BUSHES

The lone hawthorn bush of the Irish countryside was also respected and feared. No one dared cut it down for fear of retribution. Even as late as the 1960s, it was not at all unusual for new roads to be rerouted because workmen refused to build through a fairy fort. As recently as 1999, the NRA changed the route of the Ennis, County Clare bypass following a successful campaign by local storyteller and folklorist, Eddie Lenihan.

Lenehan claimed that a lone hawthorn bush at Latoon, near Newmarket-on-Fergus, marked the site where the fairies of Munster gathered before they set out to do battle with the fairies of Connacht. It is also the place where the ghostly 'Dead Hunt' passes through. 'They would be vexed by the removal of their bush and when they are vexed they have no mercy,' an unapologetic Lenihan argued.

It has also been claimed that a fairy fort was demolished for the controversial Quarryvale Shopping Centre development in Dublin, which in turn precipitated the Mahon tribunal.

Back in the '50s, a Bunduff man, Hugh Feeney, was warned by neighbours to leave the fairy fort and bush on his land alone. Unfortunately, according to my neighbour Bernie K-----, he didn't heed the warnings:

> I used to be without rambling with Hugh Feeney, poor devil, an ye couldn't go in to a nicer man on a Sunday. He got this Donegal man out with his digger. He cleaned and levelled before him. I said, 'That bush was there before you an' before yer father. They made a living without ever going near it, if I was you I'd lave it alone.'
> 'That's all rubbish,' says Hugh.
>
> I was without one evening, ramblin' with him; we were very great, we were friends. He was at the tay when I went in, he offered me a mug

but I didn't need it. The poor fellow didn't have half the cup of tay taken when he had to go down to the door and he caught a holt of the jambs that way and his head was nearly taking the ground with a vomit.

'Hugh,' says I, 'ye failed greatly since the last time I was talking to you.'

'I'm finished, Bernie,' he says, 'I'm going away for Dublin shortly, I have the boyo.'

He went away for Dublin an' never came back. My sister was living in Dublin. She went in to see him, she wouldn't go back a second time. He was that far gone ye couldn't look at him. That wasn't long after he did the work.

A hawthorn bush along Pat Leonard's ditch was in John Hannon's way. When he was cutting the bush, oul' Pat Leonard came out to him, 'Do you know what ye'll do John, lave that bush where it is. I never seen that bush a setting ever. Lave it there an it'll do you no harm.'

'Oh I won't be long cutting it down, Pat, wait yet, I'm going to cut it down one way or another, it's a bloody nuisance coming and going here.'

When he was cutting the bush, didn't it cut him in the face, three days after he was away for Dublin – never came back. That's the truth, there's no fairy tales about that!

On a visit to Tom Leonard of Grange, he told me that 'Benbulben School is built on a fort'.

When they were widening the road there at that time nobody would touch it at all. The engineer went in an' started an dug the first bit. He fell down steps about a month afterwards and broke his neck. Whoever touches the first sod the curse'll be on them. Another man C. McG, his father, was cleaning out a fort, the next thing he got a stroke. He only lived about six weeks after it.

Many locals have their own tales recalling the consequences of interfering with the fairies, such as this one by Johnny McGowan.

I know a man in this country an' and he lost all his hair almost overnight an people were wondering at it. There was a fort in the field. 'That fella,' I said, 'went up the field an' he cut all the bushes in the forth out of it, left it bare, there was a lovely ring of blackthorn around the forth. A few months after that he hadn't a wisp on his head, it was as clean as a football. The bucks came at him.'

Ye can see it, ye can folly it up, but there's no good telling the people that's going now about that.

An' it's still happening! There was another man then an' there was a fort above at Kilmacannon, above at the back of his house on D----'s land. M------ got a Hymac into it and he flittered the whole lot out an' he levelled it. About a week after that the cows took BSE an' it was only weeks before there wasn't a four-legged animal on the farm. That's the truth. It happened several times around here.

J.P. Lenehan recalled:

Down in Lissadell there's a lot of stone circles. I was working for the Land Commission and we were working at houses over round about there. There was this place we were sent to and it was a ring fort. We levelled it anyway. Begod the first thing that happened I got a stob on the hand and it swelled up. Another of the fellows fell into a septic tank and nearly drowned. There was a man working with Jose S------, ... didn't his health go down. Another of the fellows was with us T---- S------ I think it was, fell down off one of the houses, and all this happened a short time after we tossed the fort.

I am much indebted to Mary Doddy of Ballymote, who introduced me to her uncle Jimmy McGettrick, an accomplished musician and *sean-chai*. He was an inspiration both in style and repertoire to Matt Molloy of The Chieftains, who spent countless hours listening to, and learning from him. Molloy's granduncle, Batty O'Hara, was from the area.

On one of my visits to Jimmy, he brought me down to a fort near his house. It was in clear view of the enchanted Keash Hill. We sat on the grassy bank encircling the fort, Jimmy and I, on a pleasant June day while he regaled me with stories of long ago. A musician of note, in between stories he would take out his tin whistle and play a few reels and jigs. Local people often heard music in that spot, he told me. It was an enchanted place, he said, and indeed as I look back on that afternoon, to sit there with Jimmy was an enchantment all its own.

Before mowing machines, he said, people mowed the meadows with scythes. It was well known that a local mowyer often tried to mow inside the fort as there was good grass on it, but he didn't like to do it as his work slowed down to a crawl while he was in there. He 'could make no headway' and yet grass was scarce, so he always persevered.

One day, tired out from mowing, he left down the scythe to have a smoke of his pipe. Taking the pipe out he left it down beside him and commenced to cut up the plug of tobacco with his knife. When he was finished he put his hand down for the pipe but, to his great surprise, it wasn't there.

'He looked and looked,' said Jimmy, 'and he couldn't find it, and him just after leaving it down out of his hand.'

'Eventually he gave up and went home to get his other pipe. When he was there he made himself a cup of tea and had a good smoke afterwards. When he came back to the fort what do you think but there was the pipe, exactly where he had left it, in plain view beside the blade of the scythe.'

'What would ye make of that?' says Jimmy. 'Wouldn't ye think that the fairies took the pipe for a smoke and when they were finished they left it back?'

Having a first-rate edge on a scythe was essential to a good mowyer. Achieving this was an art in itself and not everyone was a master of it. One of the methods by which the fairies protected their property, some believed, was by 'taking the edge off the scythe'. This could be prevented by hanging a rosary beads on the scythe blade when not in use.

CALLED OUT AT NIGHT

'It's a dangerous business, Frodo, going out your door. You step onto the road, and if you don't keep your feet, there's no knowing where you might be swept off to.'

(J.R.R. Tolkien, *The Fellowship of the Ring*)

Long ago, when the fairies were more active than they are now, and when people were more honest than they are now, doors were left open at night. However, if you heard a voice calling in the darkness outside it was wise not to answer it. Not until you were called three times.

It was a common belief that the fairies were often up to their mischief at night and if you answered they had you.

However, even if the worst happened and you were taken to their abode, it was well known that if you ate or drank nothing there, they had no more power over you. There was a man went out once after being called and the fairies took him away. He met a girl on the way and she told him: 'Eat nothing from them and drink nothing, for if you do, you'll never get back. He did that and they had to let him go. He was away a whole night with them.'

LED ASTRAY BY THE FAIRIES

There are a few wayfarers left who can still tell hair-raising stories of being 'put astray' by a mischievous act of the fairies, making them lose their sense of direction, and wander lost till morning. Unless ... unless, they were wise in country ways ...

Paddy F------ of Derelehan, a man who knew every rock and gully on the Sligo mountains, had a close call when he was put astray:

Out on the mountain I had a dog with me and a pup as well. An' the oul' dog, well she was as clever! She was going in the right direction when the fog came down but I thought she was wrong and I called her back. When I realised I was astray I knew I was in the 'fairy courses' then. Ye know it by the ground, ye rub yer fingers like that on the wee stuff that grows on the top of it. I could go out yet an' show it to ye, where these fairy courses are. It's not a real grass, it's a bluey kind of a thin wiry grass. It grows in patches, like a round circle. I sat down for a good while until I started to get cold. I spent the night on the mountain anyway, an' I travelled 4 miles away from home. I ended up on Barnaribbon mountain when it was clearing day. Of course I had a stroke of luck that I didn't come in on the top

of a cliff and fall over. That could have happened too when ye can't
see where you're going and it'd be the end of me!

***

It happened once to my neighbour, Bernie Kelly. The experience etched
itself so strongly on his being that he remembered the incident in every
detail. When he told me what happened, it was so fresh in his mind that
it was as if it took place yesterday:

> It was during the war years, money was scarce then and five shillings a
> pair for the rabbits was good money, we were glad to get it. We had a
> great wee hound here and the Conway's had a wee white dog – he was a
> nailer. Four of us arranged to go out this night anyway, there was Boyce
> in it and Thady Conway, meself and the brother Dan. We had carbide
> lamps with us an' they were that strong they'd cut th' eyes out of yer
> head. We headed away for the Wee Burra, the rabbits were plentiful and
> we had six or seven killed in no time. We went out to the racecourse – it
> was staked that time to keep foreign planes from landing during the
> war. We killed a few more rabbits there and, begod, when we went to
> come out of the racecourse, we couldn't get out of it! There was water all
> around us no matter which way we went – the channel was all round us,
> the sea was below us and the Brook on th' other side.
>
> The four of us went together first an' when that didn't do any good
> Thady an' me kept one side and Thomas Boyce and Dan took the
> other side an' still we couldn't get out – water in front of us no matter
> where we went. Thomas says to me then, 'I can tell ye now we're here
> till morning. This happened to meself and Tommy Fowley one time
> before and we couldn't make our way out till it broke day.'
>
> It didn't look good, but I was lucky; I remembered I heard Paddy
> Barry telling me father one time that he was put astray one morning
> coming home from Mac Barry's, his brother's house. I was small at
> the time but I was listening to them talking and remembered Paddy
> saying that he turned his coat inside out an' that's how he got home.
> If ye turn yer coat or cap, it has the power to break the spell. That or
> the cock crowing in the morning will do it too.

Thady an' meself said we'd try to get out one more time so out and around we went again, an' still no use. We still couldn't find a way out!

'Do you know what I'll do now,' says I to Thady, 'I'll turn me coat inside out an' see if it does any good.'

I turned the coat inside out, put it back on me and, I'm telling no lie, we didn't walk twenty yards until we were on the race course, the sticks was there and I could see everything before us. We called the other fellas, they were still on the other side of the channel but they came to the sound of our voices and made their way out too.

'Do ye know what we'll do?' says Thomas, 'Make for the gatehouse an' we'll get out on the road an' go home.'

That's what we did an' if ye think I'm telling a lie now, Thomas is above there in the house, ye can go up and ask him an' he'll tell you the same thing I'm telling ye. I used to laugh at Paddy Barry when he'd tell us about being put astray, but I was laughing the other side of my face that night, I'll tell ye!

Bernie had fallen victim to the 'shaughran' or *seachran sidhe* (fairy wandering). It was an enchantment that caused travellers to lose their way on paths and in fields well known to them. Mischievous fairies were held responsible and no one ever came to any harm.

***

As with every theory and custom, there were the believers and unbelievers, the doubters and the defiant: Pat Dan and Paddy McSharry, two Cliffoney men, out rambling to a neighbour's house, took a shortcut home across a commonage known as Parkes' Farm. They chatted as they walked across fields they had travelled innumerable times before. On this night, however, things took a different turn. No matter which way they walked, or how far, it was to no avail; they could not find their way home. They tried and retried, they went this way and that – but it was no good. Familiar fields and paths looked unfamiliar to them, as if they were in a strange land. Finally it dawned on them that they had somehow, some way, been put astray. McSharry, having heard others describe similar experiences, suggested that they take their coats off and turn them inside out to break the spell. Pat Dan was having none of it: 'I'll see them in hell before I'd give them the satisfaction' was his indignant reply, as he prepared to sit it out till morning.

At the first dawn glimmering, they heard a cock crow in the distance, paths and ditches were slowly revealed and the proud and the defiant made their way home without any concession whatsoever to the fairies.

Should we scoff at these beliefs? Scorn the storyteller?

'Oh day and night but this is wondrous strange,' Horatio said of the apparition of the king of Denmark's ghost in Shakespeare's *Hamlet*.

'And therefore as a stranger give it welcome,' was Hamlet's reply. 'There are more things in heaven and earth, Horatio, than are dreamt of in your philosophy'.

We must admit that strange and unexplainable things do occur. Credible witnesses tell of inexplicable experiences in every detail. There are times when even the most hardened sceptic must allow that there are occurrences, like the *seachran,* for which we have no rational explanation.

'But how is it these things don't happen today?' I hear you say.

'When is the last time you walked home across the fields from a neighbour's house as people did long ago?' I ask. Perhaps we don't disturb the fairies any more in their nocturnal comings and goings, and consequently they don't have an opportunity to bother us.

***

Although stories like these were common currency around the fireside not so long ago, many today will question whether these Otherworld people ever existed. Like the man who was asked if he believed in them, we may disclaim loudly that we could never be so credulous. 'Believe in them,' he declared, 'of course not – but they're there just the same!'

STRAY SOD

The 'stray sod' or *fóidín mearbhaill* was another hazard that added to travellers' confusion. During famine times, when people died in great numbers, the remains were carried long distances overland to be buried. It is said that the sward where the coffins were put down to rest became the 'stray sod'. Ever after, anyone taking a shortcut across fields at night that stepped on this piece of ground was liable to be 'put astray'.

It happened to a County Sligo family in the famine year of 1848. There was no food in the sod house where Grace W. lived with her mother along the River Easkey. Begging was futile as the neighbours had nothing to eat either.

To put the times in context, some time previously a man by name of McManus was found nearby, lying in a drain. The person who found him went to two or three houses to see if someone would take him in. The residents refused, afraid that he was infected with typhus fever. Placing him on straw in a haggard overnight, McManus's rescuer returned in the morning to find him dead and 'dreadfully mutilated'.

An inquest, held on 12 January and reported in the *Sligo Champion* of 16 January 1847, showed that 'both the legs, as far as the buttocks, appeared to have been eaten off by a pig; I [the coroner] am of the opinion his death was caused by hunger and cold. There was not a particle of food found in deceased's stomach or intestines.' Those who saw the body were of the opinion, from the agonized expression on McManus's face, that he was alive when the pig devoured him.

It was against this terrible background that Grace's mother died of hunger. Her daughter 'was in a terrible way':

> … she had no money or any means to buy a coffin in which to bury her mother. She thought of a plan. She put the corpse into a creel and carried it on her back to Kilmacshalgan old Churchyard where she buried the remains. On her way to the Churchyard she laid down the creel a few times to rest. To this day it is believed there is a 'stray' in the places where she rested the creel. It is said that any place a corpse is rested there is always a stray in that place.

Oaten bread was a staple food of the Irish countryside at one time and was taken to mountain, bog and fair. When the fair was held in a distant town, farmers 'had to leave home very early in the morning, five or six o'clock. Maybe stand at a fair all day long then an' ye mightn't sell or have anything to eat an' walk back home again in the evening. If ye had a bit of oatcake in your pocket, there was great support in it,' Mickey Mc Groarty once told me. He went on to tell me about other uses to which oatmeal cake was put:

> People going away on a journey out the mountains to look about sheep always put a bit of oatbread in their pocket – ye'd never get hungry when ye'd have it. The reason people took it in their pocket was this: ye could be up in the middle of them hills an' suddenly ye could drop down from hunger with a *Féar Gortach*, a weakness ye got, right all of a sudden.

This is how the *Féar Gortach* came about, as explained to me by Mickey: in the old days the houses were way far apart and the burial grounds was even further away.

> [If a neighbour died] way back in one o' them remote districts where they were living, they were carried through the fields, as often there was no road. A crew of fifteen or sixteen men took turns carrying the coffin, four men carrying at any one time. When they got tired they would leave it down to rest and maybe take a smoke before they went on another bit. In the famine times they couldn't keep up, there was that many dying. Wherever they left the coffin down, from that time on it was known as a stray sod so when you stepped on this you got the *Féar Gortach*. If ye stepped on it at night ye were put astray, too. It was given to that! If ye had a bit of oat bread in yer pocket ye'd be safe.

The *Féar Gortach* or 'hungry grass' was well known not just in Sligo but all over Ireland. It looks no different from any other grass but is believed to grow on the spot, as Mickey explained, where some poor person died on the *Casán na Marbh* or Path of Death during the great famine.

> Crossing the shallow holdings high above sea
> Where few birds nest, the luckless foot may pass

From the bright safety of experience
Into the terror of the hungry grass.

Here in a year when poison from the air
First withered in despair the growth of spring
Some skull-faced wretch whom nettle could not save
Crept on four bones to his last scattering.

Crept, and the shrivelled heart which drove his thought
Towards platters brought in hospitality
Burst as the wizened eyes measured the miles
Like dizzy walls forbidding him the city.

Little the earth reclaimed from that poor body
And yet remembering him the place has grown
Bewitched and the thin grass he nourishes
Racks with his famine, sucks marrow from the bone.

- Donagh Mc Donagh, 'The Hungry Grass'

There are very few who having worked at turf or hay, on bog or field, have not experienced the sudden, unreasonable craving of hunger that Mickey describes. Some attribute this to a sudden drop in blood sugar levels. Doctors dispute this but cannot assign the condition to any known medical factor. If this is so, then Mickey's explanation is as good as any. Whatever the reason, many who feared its effects carried a bit of oat bread or such in their pocket, knowing from experience that any small amount of food helped to relieve the condition.

My first experience with the *Féar Gortach* was on Cloonerco bog many years ago while 'capping' and spreading turf. My father cut the dark sods with the turfspade and slung them towards me in a steady rhythm: cut, lift, swing, throw, catch. Suddenly, and for no apparent reason, my legs became weak and shaky and a feeling of great hunger overwhelmed me. It was early in the day but I hesitantly suggested to my father that it was time to light the fire and put the kettle on. He was always the final arbiter of the work and meal schedule, and fair – by his standards. 'What's wrong with ye? Sure, we only got here,' he said, raising his eyebrows as he scanned an anxious face. Knowing that dinner and tea were my favourite times of day, any day, he was suspicious. 'That's the *Féar Gortach* ye have', he said finally when I explained to him the ravenous hunger that had come over me. 'When ye step on the hungry grass, that's what happens. It's a bit early for eating yet, but go ahead.'

A resident of nearby Ballintrillick explained to me another method of overcoming the effects of 'Hungry Grass': 'If ye stoop down an' get a bit of a sally bush, ye know the *raideog*, the wee low sally bush that grows in them places, put it in yer mouth – the fact that ye chewed or let down the saliva would cure the *Féar Gortach*.'

Some attributed the sudden hunger to the power of the fairies. Seamus McManus in his book, *Bold Blades of Donegal*, explained it as a bewitched grass that was once sat upon by greedy people who ate their fill without leaving a bit for the 'Gentle People', or fairies. In olden times the fairies demanded their share of whatever was going, be it milk, or *poitín*, or in this case food.

The Borrowed Child

'An uncle of mine told me this and swore it was as true as the gospel,' Paddy L----- of Derelehan informed me.

It was supposed to have happened not too far away from around here, I wouldn't like to say:

This fellow was coming home late one night from rambling on a November night. As he passed by this house the window opened and a child was passed out through it to him. 'Here she is,' said the individual that handed out the child. He took the child in his arms and brought her home. He hadn't far to go. When he told the wife, she said, 'In the name of God, where did you get the child?' He told her and she responded, 'Why did you take it?'

'I didn't like not to,' he said, 'because whoever handed it out was waiting for someone to come.'

'Go back with it,' she said, 'and leave it where you got it.'

'No,' says he, 'put it in a wee cot or basket and we'll keep it for the night.' And so they did.

In the morning, the next-door neighbour came roaring and crying to their house, saying her child was dead. Yer man looked at his wife and he shook his head. The woman kept crying and crying about the child being dead. He took his wife aside and he said, 'Don't show her that child, leave that child there. Sit the woman down and try and pacify her. I'm going back to their house.'

He went to the house and there was a great fire on. He looked at the man, who was in a bad way, and the dead child and he lifted it up in his hands like that. The next thing was didn't he catch it by the breast and went down to the fire, held it out an yer man nearly thrappled him ye know, to go burning the child.

As soon as he dropped it into the fire, it drew wan squawk out of it an' it went out the chimney like a bird. He told the man: 'Yer child is alright, I took it home last night. There must be witchcraft in this thing because it wouldn't be fairycraft.'

They used to say that time that the witch would try to get someone into the house under cover anonst of the people that were there.

OBSTRUCTED BY THE FAIRIES

On one of my visits to Jimmy McGettrick he told me of a few neighbours, who shall remain nameless here, that were visiting one night in D----'s house. There was a child there in the cradle that they were looking after. After they were in the house for a while, they came to notice that there was something different about it. They couldn't put their finger on it, but it didn't seem like an ordinary child. As well as it being irritable, the baby never seemed to settle down, cried continuously and seemed to have extraordinary strength for a child only a few months old. Soon they began to wonder if it was a changeling. It being so restless, they were concerned and, fearing it would topple out on to the floor, secured it to the cradle.

Some time after that, they heard that the child had passed away. Mourners and family had to go through a narrow pass in order to get to the main road. When the coffin was being brought out, it could not be brought through the pass. There was no obstruction, nor anything physical that impeded it, but still it could not be brought through. A few neighbours decided to head up to Bunninadden for the priest to see if he could do something. On arriving, the priest commenced to pray and it was only then that the family could proceed with the coffin.

Afterwards, people puzzled as to how or why such a strange and unusual incident could occur. They were told by the older members of the community, wise in such matters, that when the fairies took a child, they wouldn't want it to have a Christian burial. Hence the difficulty in bringing the child to consecrated ground.

GIFTS AND TALENTS FROM THE FAIRIES

'You have burnt all the witches,' the poet W.B. Yeats accused the Scots.

> In Ireland we have left them alone. To be sure the 'loyal minority' knocked out the eye of one with a cabbage-stump on the 31st of March, 1711, in the town of Carrickfergus. But then the 'loyal minority' is half Scottish. You have discovered the faeries to be pagan and wicked. You would like to have them all up before the magistrate. In Ireland warlike mortals have gone among them, and helped them in their battles, and they in turn have taught men great skill with herbs, and permitted some few to hear their tunes.[20]

The fairies, although sometimes mischievous, are never vindictive. It is well known that from time to time they can be quite benevolent and are more than generous in the endowment of their gifts on mortals. These are only a few instances of many I have come across over the years.

***

Mickey Gilgan of Drumcliffe, although having no formal veterinary qualifications, was highly regarded throughout the countryside for his powers in curing cattle. Even hard cases that had been given up by veterinarians were cured by his gift. As is traditional with people who possess these special gifts, he never charged but would accept some small gift of tobacco or such.

My family had personal experience of his skill when a valuable milk cow we had could not rise shortly after calving. The vet had failed, as did neighbours, who had tried to raise the animal with ropes and bags. My mother, having heard of Gilgan, cycled over to his house. She told me how it went:

When I got there, I had to wait as he was out fishing on the river.
It ran by close to his house. When he got back, I explained about the
cow. He listened very carefully and asked a few questions. He went
up to his room then and was there for a good while, saying prayers
maybe, I don't know. When he came down, he told me to go home
and when I got there, the cow would be better. He told me to give
her a bucket and a half of mangolds and an armful of hay after that.
He said he liked people to come back to tell him if his cures worked.

When I got back home, sure enough it was like he said, the cow
was standing up! I couldn't believe my eyes. Your father went right
away and sliced the mangolds and got an armful of hay and fed it
to the cow. She was cured exactly as he said she would be. How he
managed to do it, I don't know. That cow never gave us a day's bother
after that. She was a one of our best milkers and would have been a
great loss if she died.

There were many such examples of Gilgan's powers throughout the
countryside. A neighbour, Thomas Boyce, had a cow with a similar
complaint. He told me all about how she was cured:

This cow we had was lying in a corner of Doyle's field. She lay there
for several days and all efforts to get her to rise failed. Gilgan was sent
for and he came out to where the cow lay. He spoke softly to her, 'Poor
lassie, poor lassie, what's wrong with ye.' He walked around her and,
going over to the ditch, he pulled some green grass and offered it to her,
talking to her all the time. This continued for about an hour and then
he pulled an armful of hay and threw it at her head: 'That's enough
now,' he said sharply to her, 'it's time for you to get up. Go on!'

The cow rose, walked down the field and right away started to
graze as if there wasn't a thing wrong with her.'

There are two theories as to how these powers were acquired. Mickey
liked to fish and spent much of his time down by the river that ran
close to his house. After his mother passed away – both his parents died
young – it is said that she appeared to him late one evening when he
was fishing. She was concerned that he was wasting his time, and that

he would always be poor by just selling the few fish he caught. Advising him that he would be better off curing cattle for farmers, she left as mysteriously as she had come.

Another version, and the reason it is included here, is that he was given a gift by the fairies. They visited him down by the river and gave him a red flannel cloth and the gift of curing. It was known that he did indeed have such a cloth and knelt on it out of sight in his bedroom as part of the curing ritual when people visited with news of a sick animal.

Whatever the reason, or how they were acquired, his healing powers were a great boon to the people of Sligo at a time in our history when there was very little money in people's pockets for essentials, let alone having sufficient to pay for professionals in times of crisis.

His little family home is still there by the Drumcliffe River, relatively unchanged from the time when he lived there. Little do passers-by know today of the remarkable man who once lived there, of the great gift he possessed or how popular he once was in the Irish countryside.

A FAMOUS SLIGO MUSICIAN

Michael Coleman, the most influential traditional Irish musician of all time, was born in the townland of Knockgrania, Killavil, County Sligo on 31 January 1891. His father, a small farmer, was James Coleman from Banada in County Roscommon, close to the Sligo border. He married Beatrice (Beesey) Gorman, a local woman from Knockgrania where they established their home.

Of Michael's music it has been said that it was impossible to play better and still be mortal. There may have been some truth in this assertion as it has been claimed that he did indeed learn his craft from the fairies. The 78rpm records made by Michael Coleman between 1921 and 1936 set the standard for Irish traditional fiddle style and repertoire in both his native Ireland and the United States. Willie Clancy, the famous piper of County Clare, when once asked his opinion on Irish traditional music replied: 'The standards are set. As far as fiddle playing goes, you can ask anyone all over Ireland and he will refer you to Sligo. Can you pass the master, Michael Coleman? I haven't many of his records but I heard quite a few and it is the *"Ceol Draoichta"* as is said in West Clare – the fairy music – that's what I think of Michael Coleman's music.'

Sligo fiddler Fred Finn recalled that Jim Coleman, Michael's brother, told his father Mick Finn, how it came about. Fred Finn then passed the story on to local historian P.J. Duffy who told me about it:

The two brothers, Michael and Jim, were returning from a night out when on the way home they went astray. Finding an old ringfort they rested there. Suddenly they were surrounded by a beautiful field 'with lovely plains, trees and flowers'. Feeling a compulsion to play they uncased their fiddles, sat down on a stone and started into a few tunes. They played on and on all night long as if enchanted and then, tired of playing, they set out again to find their way home. When they arrived at their house they were astonished to find that it was still early in the night and they were only ten minutes late.

From then on, 'it was noticed in the houses round about where they used to play that there was a remarkable improvement in their music. Jim was terrified to go out at night all his life after that.' Indeed it has often been claimed that Jim was an even better player than Michael but as Jim never emigrated he remained unknown to fame.

The opportunities for Michael to earn a living from his music in Sligo were small. After trying his hand at some part time jobs and after a brief stay with one of his brothers in England, Michael decided to leave Sligo. He sailed to America in 1914, arriving at Ellis Island on 1 November 1914. Initially, Michael stayed with his aunt in Lowell, Massachusetts.

Between 1921 and 1936 he recorded eighty 78rpm records for many record labels, including: Shannon, Vocalion Records, Columbia Records, Okeh Records, New Republic, Pathé, O'Beirne de Witt, Victor Records, Brunswick Records, and Decca Records. He was mainly accompanied by pianists, but on some recordings he used guitarists.

In 1974, a monument was erected by the Coleman Traditional Society. It is close to his birthplace, on the Tubbercurry to Gurteen road. Nearby is the Coleman Heritage Centre, a music archive and a replica of the house where he lived. The monument bears this inscription: 'Michael Coleman. Master of the fiddle. Saviour of Irish traditional music. Born near this spot in 1891. Died in exile 1945.'

THE PIPER'S LOSS

If the fairies could give gifts to mortals, it seems they could equally take them away. Such was the case with a piper, who lived at one time in Dromore West, County Sligo. He was invited to all the dances around and, as a consequence, was often out late at night. It happened on one November night he was playing at a dance in a country house. Returning home that night – or the early hours of the morning – he found that the roads were dark, there were no lights in the windows and everyone was in bed. As he came around a bend, he noticed a light on the hillside and, curious about it, decided to go have a look to see who was up at that hour. Maybe there was another dance and sure he was in no hurry home.

Going up to the hill, he saw what looked like a very fine mansion. He stood there, scratching his head and wondered why he had not seen this building before. Suddenly, the front door opened in a blaze of light, a crowd of dwarfish men rushed out and, surrounding him, examined his pipes with great curiosity. With them was a beautiful woman dressed in a very fancy gown. The group coaxed and pleaded with him to come in. He was somewhat afraid of the strange-looking group but finally consented to go in anyway. Once inside, he was greeted with great enthusiasm. What a welcome he got!

Placing him at the head of the table, the gathering clamoured for him to play the uilleann pies that he carried in an old bag. Pleased to be asked and beginning to enjoy the jolly company, he played reels, jigs and hornpipes to beat the band. He played on and on, and the people on the floor danced and danced until finally the piper got so tired he could play no more. He could hardly lift his arms, he was that exhausted.

The woman he had met outside came to him and asked if he would play on as a special favour to her. He refused, saying that he had been playing all night and couldn't manage another tune. She begged and pleaded but it was to no avail; he simply couldn't play another tune. Never having been refused before, she grew very angry, retorting: 'You dare to refuse me, the Queen of the Fairies! Now you will never play another note. You might have the music but I have the tune.'

Turning on her heel, she walked away from him. The piper, sorry now that he had not agreed to play, said that if she would come back, he would play a few more tunes. He had, however, missed his opportunity. The Queen's helpers showed him to his bedroom. Taking off his clothes, he recalled later that he hung them on what seemed like golden pegs.

When he awoke in the morning, he was lying under a hawthorn bush with his clothes hanging from the branches. Had he dreamed all of this? Remembering the Queen's threat, he took his beloved pipes out to play but not a note would come. It was as the Fairy Queen had told him: from that day on, not a note could he ever play again.

AWAY WITH THE FAIRIES

A man was once taken away for a ride with the fairies. There was a girl getting married and the fairies could not take her without having a human with them, so the fairies went in to a loft over the kitchen and brought the man with them, warning him to be quiet and not say a word. When the girl was dancing, they touched her nose with a *traithnín* (wisp) and she began to sneeze. Before she sneezed for the third time, the man forgot himself and said 'God bless us', and with that all the fairies left like a blast of wind, leaving him alone. He got to leave the house without anyone seeing him. He kept on walking till the next morning and he saw a girl milking a cow, so he stopped and asked her if he was far from Ballyfarnon. She said she heard of Ballyfarnon only once in her life, when her master mentioned a fair that was held there. After walking for many days, the man finally arrived home.

A FAIRY STORY

Two men were putting in hay one bright moonlit night. One of the men returned to the haggard with the cartload of hay while the other one stayed behind. He took out his pipe and lit it, and what appeared but several young ladies with fiddles. They began to play and dance around him. This was at around twelve o'clock at night. He got afraid for his life and lay down on the cock. After a while the other man came back. They filled another load and the man that stayed the last time went in with the load this time. He too took out his pipe for a smoke. As soon as he struck the match this young lady came up and asked him if he had another. They started to play and dance around him as before. He lifted a layer of the hay cock and hid under it. They went up on the top of the hay and continued to dance and play. This man stayed very quiet until the other man came back and he said: 'We'll bring no more hay in tonight for I'm half killed already for such dancing and playing I never heard before. The two men started off for home with the cart empty. The fairies laughed and played away.

THE LEPRECHAUN

The Leprechaun is a very tiny person, wears a green cap and red coat. His chief occupation is making and mending shoes for the fairies. He is said to sit on a toadstool and can be heard tapping after dark, making shoes for the fairies.

The leprechaun is a very friendly person and all of them know where a crock of gold is hidden. Whatever lucky person catches one he should not let him go until he tells you where it is.

Once upon a time there lived a poor woman and her son in a small hut. They were very poor and the son was always wishing that one day he would catch a leprechaun. Late one evening as he was bringing in the cows he suddenly heard a tapping behind him. He looked around and there was a leprechaun mending shoes. He put out his hand and caught him. The Leprechaun struggled fiercely to free himself but the lad would not let him go. He asked him where is the crock of gold hidden?

The Leprechaun pretended he did not know what gold was. After some persuasion he offered to tell the boy where a crock of gold was hidden so the boy took off his tie, tied it around the little fellow and led him along. The Leprechaun kept running through hedges so it was no easy job for the boy to keep up with him till at last he stopped in a field of thistles. The Leprechaun said it is under the tallest thistle in the middle of the field that it was hidden. So the boy took out a

red cloth out of his pocket and left it on the thistle. He put the leprechaun into his pocket and started home to get a spade to dig it up.

When he arrived home there was no Leprechaun in his pocket.
He had vanished from sight but the boy did not mind as he had left
the red cloth on the thistle. He headed out for the field but when he
arrived there all the thistles in the field were covered in red cloths.
Just then nearby he heard the tapping of a hammer and he heard the
Leprechaun singing a merry song as if he enjoyed the joke he played
on the boy.[21]

25

WINTER'S
TALES

Ever wonder how people passed the long winter nights years ago
without radio, television, or any other electronic diversions?

'Rambling', or 'ceilidhing' to a neighbour's house was the custom
throughout the winter months until the middle of the twentieth
century. In every town and village there were storytellers born with
the gift to enthrall. Claypipe smoking was a fashionable virtue then
and an integral part of storytelling. It was a social ritual that bonded
friendships, relaxed the audience and mellowed the atmosphere.
The American Indian may have had his peace pipe but the Irish had
their friendship pipe. Memories sharpened and visions danced in
the blue haze and spiralling smoke rings. The world outside ceased
to exist; fact and fantasy merged and followed the pungent fumes in
ethereal flight. A theatre of the heart, hearth and home lit only by a
candle or oil lamp. As with Mickey McGroarty on a previous page,
Maggie McGowan captured for me the ambience of such a long ago
night-time fireside:

Maggie, originally from Teesan, just north of the town of Sligo,
recalled how her father would 'fill his pipe with tobacco. He'd light it,
take a pull, wipe the shank on a corner of his coat and pass it on to the
next man. He'd clean it the same way till all had a pull and then the
stories'd start. 'Twas a grand old custom,' she declared.

Here, then, are a few of these old stories.

CATS IN THE BARN

There were two men: a landlord, Sir Robert, and his tenant, who became embroiled in a big argument. The tenant maintained that religion was the most important thing in a man's life, while the landlord insisted that riches were. The argument escalated into a bitter fight between the two men, which resulted in the landlord striking the tenant with his whip, blinding him in both eyes. The man – Diarmuid was his name – was distraught as now he wouldn't be able to till his little plot of land or feed his family; it was late in the evening and, unable to make his way home, he lay down in a hay barn.

After a long time, and in great pain, he fell asleep. He was awakened at about midnight by a big commotion going on in the barn. He heard a whole lot of cats coming in the door, while three more were putting down a fire. He couldn't see them but heard the sound of the flames and the cats blowing on the fire to kindle it. Diarmuid listened and, frightened half to death, hardly dared to breathe as all the cats sat around the fire.

After a while, one of them stood up and said: 'The daughter of the High King of Ireland is very sick he has promised half of his kingdom to anyone who would make his daughter well.'

'You know,' said another cat, 'these humans are very stupid, they think they know everything but there is a way to cure her.'

'Aye,' said another,' you'd think if they knew anything they'd know that there's a well outside of Cloonacool a few miles out the road from Tubbercurry that will cure all ills and blemishes. It's cats that know everything, not humans. We have the power.'

Diarmuid listened to all this with great interest. He lay awake all night, afraid that if he slept that he would snore, and something told him that these cats wouldn't like it if they knew they were being overheard. When the cats left in the morning, he made his way to the well. Splashing the water on his eyes, he found that his sight was restored instantly. 'The cats are right,' he thought, 'there's a great cure in this water.'

Finding an old bottle, he filled it with water from the well and, mindful of the information he had overheard, made his way to the King's castle. Arriving there, he announced that he had a cure and had come to heal the King's daughter. Normally the King's retainers wouldn't give much of a hearing to a commoner, but knowing that the King was desperate for a remedy, they took him to the Princess. Propping her up on a pillow, for she was very weak and her eyes closed, he coaxed her to trust him and take a few sips from the bottle. This she did and soon she opened her eyes, stretched, got up out of bed and walked a few steps.

The King was delighted, the daughter fell in love with Diarmuid and soon they were married. Of course, now having inherited half the kingdom, Diarmuid became very rich. A year later, the landlord with whom Diarmuid had the fight, having heard all about Diarmuid's good fortune, came to visit him. Feigning friendship, he congratulated Diarmuid, telling him how pleased he was to see him doing so well.

'And tell me now, how did you manage that, Diarmuid?' he enquired craftily. Diarmuid, being an open-minded and honest fellow by nature, told him everything that had transpired; the cats, the barn and the well. That was all Sir Robert needed to know, so on arriving home, he made plans to emulate Diarmuid's good fortune. Impatiently waiting for darkness, he made his way to the barn, hid himself under an armful of hay and settled down to wait. Sure enough, on the stroke of midnight the cats came in, put down a fire and sat around talking.

'Someone must have been listening to us talking this night twelve months ago,' the biggest cat said, 'because the King's daughter is cured. No one say a word more tonight till we search the place to make sure it doesn't happen again. It'll be dear on him if we catch him!'

The cats started searching about and soon came upon the landlord hiding under the hay. There was a great flurry of snarling, scratching and spitting and when it was all over, they had torn him to bits! They ate him until there was nothing left but the shoes. That was the end of the wily landlord. His soldiers sent search parties out for him, but no one around Cloonacool or Tubbercurry ever found out what happened to the greedy landlord.

That is except for the cats, of course, who told the story to me!

HUDDEN AND DUDDEN AND DOMHNALL O'LEARY

Once upon a time there were two farming brothers, and their names were Hudden and Dudden. They had poultry in their yards, sheep on the uplands, and scores of cattle in the meadowland alongside the river. But for all that they weren't happy, for just between their two farms there lived a poor man by the name of Domhnall O'Leary. He lived in a small little house and had only a strip of grass that was barely enough to keep his one cow, Daisy, from starving. Although she did her best, it was but seldom that Donald got a drink of milk or a roll of butter from Daisy.

You would think there was little here to make Hudden and Dudden jealous, but so it is that the more one has the more one wants, and Domhnall's neighbours lay awake of nights, scheming how they might get hold of his little strip of grassland. Daisy, poor thing, they never thought of; she was just a bag of bones.

One day Hudden met Dudden, and they were grumbling away as usual, and all to the tune of 'how we could get that bucko Domhnall out of the way'.

'We'll kill Daisy,' said Hudden at last. 'If that doesn't make him clear out, nothing will. He'll have to go then.'

No sooner was it said than agreed, and it wasn't dark before Hudden and Dudden crept up to the little shed where poor Daisy lay, trying her best to chew the cud, though she hadn't had as much grass in the day as would cover your hand. When Domhnall came to see if Daisy was all snug for the night, the poor beast had only time to lick his hand once before she fell down dead. Domhnall was devastated. He thought a long time about it and finally hit on a plan. He took the hide off Daisy – it was no good to her now anyway – and was on his way to town to sell it when a magpie alighted on the hide. He caught hold of the bird and put it inside his coat. On he went then and when he reached town, he went into a public house and called for a glass of whiskey. Domhnall pressed on the bird and it let out a squeal. 'That's not your best whiskey,' said Domhnall.

The barman took it back and served a second one. Domhnall pressed on the bird again and it gave another squeal. 'That's not your best whiskey,' said Domhnall.

The barman took this one back as well and served the third glass. 'That is your best whiskey,' said Domhnall as he drank it off.

'My man,' said the barman, 'what class of a bird is that you have there?'

'That is a bird that has been in our family for generations and he is able to tell us anything we wish to know.'

'Would you sell the bird?' said he to Domhnall.

'Well,' said Domhnall, 'that's a thing I wouldn't like to do, but I am very poor and if I got a good price I might be tempted.'

After a long session of bargaining, Domhnall consented to let the bird go for £100. He drank so much whiskey then that he went home in a merry mood, singing and shouting. On his way home he met Hudden and Dudden and they were surprised to see him feeling so well and happy.

'Domhnall,' they said, 'how is it that you are in such good cheer and your cattle dead?'

'Ah!' said Domhnall, 'that was all for good luck, how I wish I had three more hides; I'd be rich for life!'

So Hudden and Dudden considered that they should kill their five cattle and sell their hides. They did so, but when they brought their hides to town they got nothing for them. On their way home they were very angry and made up their minds to kill Domhnall O'Leary.

That very night, Domhnall told his mother to sleep in his bed. Hudden and Dudden came in through the window and, knowing they were in Domhnall's room, killed the old woman, thinking that she was Domhnall.

The next day, Domhnall put his dead mother on his back and set off to town to bury her. When he came to a public house, he put her on a window stool outside, went inside and called for a glass of whiskey.

'Go out to the old woman,' said Domhnall to the barman's little daughter, 'and tell her to come in. She's a little deaf so you'll have to shout to her.'

The girl went out, spoke to the old woman and then shouted to her. There was no response, so the girl gave the woman's clothes a pluck, at which she fell over on to the street. The child, getting quite a fright, ran into the building, saying the old woman was in a faint. Everyone in the pub ran out and lifted her up, while Domhnall shouted and cried and said they had his old mother killed. She was carried inside and he could not be consoled, the poor fellow, until the barman agreed to pay him £200 and to go away and bury her quietly and to be quick about it. When it was done, Domhnall drank his fill and went home singing.

On his way home, he met Hudden and Dudden and they still more wondered and asked him how it was he was in such good humour and his mother dead!

'Ah,' said Domhnall, 'it was all for luck. On my way to bury her, I met a party of foreigners buying old hags and I got £300 for her. I wish I had another, 'tis I would go to town again and cry out, 'Old hags for sale! Old hags for sale!'

Hudden and Dudden made up their minds to kill their old mother. They did so and brought her to town crying out, 'Old hags for sale! Old hags for sale!' just like Domhnall told them.

The King's officers came along and the result was that they were arrested, tried and got three months in jail. When they were released, they made up their minds to drown Domhnall. They waited for him and, grabbing him, put him in a sack. On their way to the river, a hare crossed their path. Putting down the sack, they followed the hare. While they were away, a cattle dealer chanced to come along driving a great herd of cattle and was surprised to see the sack and a man singing inside it. The dealer walked up and asked why it was that he was singing.

'Oh, I am singing and happy, for I am on my way to heaven,' Domhnall replied.

'Oh isn't it happy for you,' the dealer said right away, 'don't I wish I was in your place.'

'Oh, then,' said Domhnall, 'you can have my place and welcome, because I can go to Heaven any day I like.'

The cattle dealer loosed the sack, let Domhnall out, and went in himself. Domhnall tied the sack, rounded up all the cattle, and set out for home with them. Hudden and Dudden came back, grabbed the sack, set out for the river and threw it in right away.

When morning came, Hudden and Dudden saw all the cattle in Domhnall's field. Filled with curiosity, they went down to the house and found Domhnall sitting comfortably by his fireside.

'We thought, Domhnall,' said they, 'that you were drowned last night.'

'So I was,' said Domhnall, 'but it was all for good luck, I'll never want. All the money and cattle a man wants is to be found at the bottom of that river!'

'Could we get money and cattle?' said they in astonishment.

'Why not?' said Domhnall, 'Go as I went.'

The two boyos thought about that information for a while and went into a sack at the river. Domhnall pushed them in, 'And there you go,' says he, 'and all my misfortune be with you.'

Domhnall came home, had their land and cattle as well as his own, and lived happily ever after.[22]

A Good Deed

John Fox, a shoemaker in Kilmacshalgan, listened in as a boy to the many stories told around the fireside by his father and neighbours who came to visit. This is one of them:

Long ago a man lived in County Sligo. He had one son and this son was a rake. His father, growing tired of his rakish ways, decided to send him out in the world and let him sink or swim. When he was going, he gave him twenty pounds and his blessing. The boy, Niall, set off and, taking ship in Sligo, set off for a far foreign land.

When he arrived at one of the South American ports, he saw a young girl tied to a stake on the top of a hill and a huge crowd of people gathered around her. He asked one of the bystanders what was the reason for the strange spectacle and the bystander told him she had disobeyed her mistress and the punishment for this was death or a fine of five pounds, which she did not have. The boy paid the fine and the girl was released. When she was let go, she came to him to thank him and said she would now follow him no matter where he went.

He told her he had neither money or means and she was very foolish to come to that decision. She replied that she did not mind about money or means but that where he went and where he got a bit she would get a bit. He then agreed to let her with him. They remained in the neighbourhood of the port till the ship was sailing to Sligo again.

In the meantime, he saw a man tied to a stake one day on the top of the same hill where he saw the girl on the day of his arrival. He again inquired the cause and he was told the man would be put to death unless he paid a fine of ten pounds. He again paid the fine and the man was released. The man came and thanked him and said that he hoped he would be able to help him some day.

Next day, the boy's ship set sail for Sligo. He and Rosie, the girl, went on, he working his way as a sailor and she helping in the cooking for the men. When they arrived in Sligo, they settled into a little house there. Rosie was an expert needlewoman, good at mending and embroidery and soon her fame spread all over the town and she got more work than she was able to do. By her skill she earned more money than was sufficient for their own needs.

One evening he came in and told her that a boat was leaving for a certain port and that he had signed on for the voyage but that she was to remain in Sligo until he returned. The night before he left, she brought him a beautifully embroidered waistcoat on which were embroidered all the birds in the air and all the fishes in the sea. She told him he was not to wear this waistcoat till he was within two days of landing and then he was to put it on. She also told him that it was her father who was inspector and harbour master in charge of that port. Part of his job was to scrutinise or examine each person as they came ashore from every ship. As each man came along her father would say, 'Stand!'

She told him he was not to halt when he said 'stand' for the first or second time but when he said, 'Stand still, my man!' he was then to stand without moving hand or foot.

When the day for sailing came, he said goodbye to her and went on board his ship. After an uneventful voyage, the ship arrived at the port. He came on shore wearing the waistcoat and was passing along, not heeding anyone. When he was ordered to stand, he took no heed. He was again ordered to stand but again took no heed of the command. Now he heard the order, 'Stand still, my man!'

On hearing this, he immediately stood facing the man who addressed him. The harbourmaster eyed Niall and asked him where

he got the waistcoat he was wearing. He replied that his wife had made it for him.

'Well,' said the harbourmaster, 'there is but one woman in the world who is able to make a waistcoat like that and she is my only daughter. I am willing to give all I possess to the man who will bring her safely back to me.'

'That's easy,' said Niall, 'since she is my wife.'

He promised to bring her with him the next time he sailed from Sligo to that port. When the boat was returning, he went back to Sligo and told his wife all that had happened.

'I expected that it would happen as it has happened,' said she.

They sold their belongings in Sligo and made ready to go on the boat to her father when it would sail again. They knew they would have plenty when they reached the port to which they were sailing, so they divided what money they possessed among the poor of the town.

They went on board and it seems they told their story to some of the sailors during the voyage. It came to the captain's ears and he immediately made plans to get rid of Niall and hand over the girl to her father and thereby reap the reward. When they were within three days sailing of the port, he threw Niall overboard, unknown to all.

Niall was a good swimmer and managed to reach a rock, where he was safe for the moment. His situation was precarious, however, as had neither water or food. The boat continued on its voyage and reached port safely. The captain handed over Rosie to her father and asked his permission to marry her. The father agreed willingly but the girl asked that the marriage should not take place for a year and a day, and this was agreed by all.

Niall clung to the rock, despairing of ever seeing land again, or seeing his wife when suddenly he saw a small boat in the distance coming towards him. As it came nearer and nearer, he noticed that it was being rowed by a black man. The boat and the man came alongside the rock. The man asked 'How much would you give to be brought to land safely?'

'What can I give when I possess nothing?' Niall replied.

'I will bring you safely to land if you promise to give me your first-born child.'

'That is impossible as I have no child, but if I ever have I promise to give him to you.'

'Then that's a bargain,' the man replied, telling him to get into the boat. Bringing him safely to land, he bade him goodbye. The sailor, Niall, now set out to find the port for which he had sailed from Sligo, hoping to find news of his wife there. A year later he reached it and found it decorated as if for some festival. Asking the reasons for the decorations and signs of rejoicing, he was told that the harbourmaster's daughter was going to be married the next day to the captain of the ship. He inquired where the bride-to-be lived and when he found out where her house was situated, he went towards it. She was sitting on a window and watching him as he approached the house.

Running out to meet him, she greeted him with great joy, welcomed him and invited him into the house. There they met her father. She told him what the captain had done and then told him how this was the man that had saved her life and that he was the one really responsible for bringing her back to him. Niall was ragged, unwashed and unshaven and looked rather a miserable sight after his year's wandering. The father, observing this, thought he was not worthy of his daughter and proposed that they should reward him and let the marriage with the captain take place as had been arranged. The girl said, 'No! Where he goes I go.'

The father, seeing what she thought of Niall, began to think that there must be more good in him than there appeared to be and consented to give him back his daughter as his true wife. Niall asked what was to be done with the captain and the father said they would burn him in a barrel of tar. Niall said that since he had come safe and since all was well and he was reunited with his wife, he didn't want revenge. He proposed that the captain should be allowed to go free. This was done and the story spread throughout the seaport. The rejoicings were held next day, not for the marriage but for the return of the man who had really brought back the lost girl and restored her to her father.

In the course of time, the couple were blest with twins. There were rejoicings again, but there was one person in the party who was troubled in his mind and that was the father of the twins. He now thought of his promise to the black man, but still he thought he had a year and a day before his promise to hand over his first-born child had to be fulfilled. He hoped against hope that in that time something might happen to free him for what he had undertaken to fulfil.

A year passed and nothing happened but the day before Niall was to fulfil his promise, his wife noticed that he was very troubled. She asked him what was wrong but no matter how she tried, he wouldn't tell her. He had never told her at any time of his promise to the man and did not intend to tell her if he could help it. She persevered and kept asking and asking and asking what was the matter with him till at last he was forced to tell her.

When she heard the story she took the matter very quietly and said, 'Oh, never mind, God will send us another to take his place.'

Next day, the day on which the promise was to be fulfilled, Niall, Rosie and their two children, dressed in their best, proceeded down the garden path to the spot where they were to meet the dark stranger. Each carried a child. When they reached the appointed place, the black man was there before them.

'Well,' he said to Niall, ' I see you are a man of your word.'

'Yes,' said Niall, 'I have always tried to keep my word, no matter what the sacrifice.'

'Are you ready now to fulfil your promise?'

'Yes,' replied Niall, 'even though it is hard to bear.'

Mother and father then kissed the child and the father handed it over. The black man next spoke and asked, 'What would you give to have your child back again?'

'Anything we possess,' replied the parents.

'Would you give £100?'

'Yes.'

'Would you give £200?'

'Yes.'

'Would you give £500?'

'Yes, and fifty times that,' replied Niall.

After a few moments pause the black man spoke and asked if Niall could ever remember doing a good deed for a man in danger. 'I don't remember,' said Niall, 'but I might have.'

'Do you remember seeing a man tied to a stake with a crowd around ready to put him to death because he could not pay a fine of ten pounds?'

'Yes,' said Niall, puzzled at where the conversation was going. 'I remember that.'

'Well, I am that man,' the stranger said, 'I saw you when you were thrown overboard, and when you climbed on to the rock. I asked as a special request from God that I would be allowed to save you because you once saved me. That request was granted to me. You have agreed that you are ready to pay ten pounds or a lot more to get your child back. You once paid ten pounds for my freedom so now here is your child back again to you and my debt is paid.'

The black man turned on his heel and, walking away, disappeared into the distance. The parents were left speechless, staring at one another and wondering if the whole thing was a dream or if what they had witnessed really happened.

Moral: A good deed never goes unrewarded.[23]

BIBLIOGRAPHY

BOOKS

Cahill, Thomas, *How the Irish Saved Civilization* (Hodder & Staughton, 1995)

Cowell, John, *Land of Yeat's Desire* (O'Brien Press, 1990)

Croker, Thomas Crofton, *Fairy Legends* (The Collins Press, 1998).

Deane, Seamus (ed.), *The Field Day Anthology of Irish Writing* (Field Day Publications, 1991)

Farry, Michael, *A Chronicle of Conflict* (Killoran Press, 1992)

Gregory, Lady, *Gods and Fighting Men* (John Murray, 1904, reprinted 1825)

Joyce, P.W., *Ancient Celtic Romances* (Parkgate Books, 1997). First published by David Nutt, 1894

Lysaght, Patricia, *The Banshee* (Roberts Rhinehart Publishers, 1986)

McGowan, Joe, *Echoes of a Savage Land* (Mercier Press, 2001)

McGowan, Joe, *In the Shadow of Benbulben* (Aeolus Publications, 1993)

McTernan, John, *At the Foot of Knocknarea* (Coolera/Strandhill GAA, 1990)

O hÓgain, Daithi, *Myth, Legend and Romance* (Ryan Publishing, 1990)

Timoney, Martin A. (ed.), *Dedicated to Sligo* (KPS Knock; Co. Mayo, 2013)

Wentz, W.Y. Evans, *The Fairy Faith in Celtic Countries* (Oxford University Press, 1911)

Wilde, F.S., *Ancient Legends, Mystic Charms and Superstitions of Ireland* (Chatto and Windus: London, 1887)

Wilde, F.S. *Ancient Legends of Ireland* (Sterling; London and New York, 1992)

Wood-Martin, W.G., *Traces of the Elder Faiths of Ireland*, Vol 1& 2 (Longmans, Green and Co., 1902)

Yeats W.B., *The Celtic Twilight* (The Guernsey Press, 1981). First published
   by Guernsey Press in 1893

WEBSITES

www.rossespointshanty.com/Heritage/coney1.htm
www.enniscrone.ie/home
www.voicesfromthedawn.com/tullaghan-hill-holy-well/

MAGAZINES/PERIODICALS/NEWSPAPERS

Corran Herald
Sligo Weekender

NOTES

1 McGowan, J., *In the Shadow of Benbulben*, p.79.

2 Many of these early texts use AM, 'in the year of the world'; dating from creation, fixed by Archbishop Ussher at 4004 BC.

3 Cahill, Thomas, *How the Irish Saved Civilization*.

4 Crying has been heard around this fort and fairies and soldiers have supposedly been seen there. According to local lore, a man cut a tree there long ago, defying the curse that, according to popular belief, falls on anyone interfering with these places: 'While he was cutting, a drop of blood splashed on his hands. Not long afterwards, he died.'

5 *The Trembling of the Veil*, p.266.

6 People believed that iron had power over the supernatural. The power of iron may be an ancestral memory of the overthrow of the Bronze Age people by the Iron Age Celts.

7 'Rambled' in this context is a colloquial term for gathering to pass the time, tell stories etc.

8 http://www.rossespointshanty.com/Heritage/coney1926.htm.

9 If the 'fairy' nets had not fouled theirs they would have stayed fishing and been drowned

10 *Corran Herald*, issue No. 32, p.8.

11 Joyce, P.W., *Joyce's History of Ancient Ireland*, Vol. 1, p.454.

12 Department of Irish Folklore, Schools Manuscript Collection.

13 Woodmartin, W.G., *Traces of the Elder Faiths of Ireland*, p.220.

14 O'Donnell, Ben, *The Story of the Rosses*, p.18-22. Sean O'Donnell or 'Sean Mac Mhanuis Óig Ó'Donnell', as he was known, was married to a sister of Brian O'Rourke of Breffni. The Annals of the Four Masters record that he killed Manus O'Donnell, a cousin of Red Hugh O'Donnell's, in 1589.

15 Adapted from Hyde, Douglas, *Legends of Saints and Sinners*, pp.127-135.

16　Joe Mc Gowan, *Echoes of a Savage Land* (Mercier Press, 2001).

17　Evans Wentz, W.Y., *The Fairy Faith in Celtic Countries.*

18　Irish folk lore, 'Lageniensis'.

19　Sullivan, Patrick V., *Irish Superstitions and Legends of Animals and Birds,* p.10; Woodmartin, W.G., *Traces of the Elder Faiths of Ireland,* Vol. 2, p.127.

20　Yeats, W.B., 'A Remonstrance with Scotsmen for having Soured the Disposition of their Ghosts and Faeries in *Mythologies,* p.107.

21　Jemyn Mary, *Irish Folklore Collection,* p.61.

22　Adapted from a story told to Máire Ní Ceallaigh by John McAndrew of Rathlee, Easkey in 1938.

23　Collected for the Irish Folklore Commission from John Fox, Kilmacshalgan, Scoil Druim Mór, Oide Seosamh Ó'Catháin, p.231.